Park
a fantastic story

JOHN GRAY

Park

a fantastic story

edited by Philip Healy

CARCANET

This edition published in Great Britain 1984
by the Carcanet Press
208 Corn Exchange Building, Manchester M4 3BQ

The Publisher acknowledges financial assistance from the
Arts Council of Great Britain

Gray, John, *1866-1934*
  Park.
  I. Title   II. Healy, P.
  823'.8 [F]   PR6013.R367

  ISBN 0-85635-538-0

Typesetting by the Yale Press, London SE25
Printed in Great Britain by SRP Ltd., Exeter

MUNGO PARK walked on in the belief, absurd as he knew it to be, that he had died. There are catastrophes (so he assured himself) where the victim need not add to his perplexity the pain of suspending his judgment. And this hypothesis was some relief to him here and now—if, as in his anguish he thought, it *is* here & *is* now. He dismissed as impertinent his own critical question: when did it happen and where and how?

One thing at a time, he answered himself. For he wanted no more than a mind sufficiently at ease to draw inferences from the evidence of his bewildered senses.

He did not deny that he felt well. All his reactions were perfect; he had no physical pain; his breathing was right; there was not the least irritation on any part of his skin; no blister, fly-bite, soreness; his clothes, hat, boots seemed ideally part of himself. His stick hung on his wrist; he could hear his watch ticking. He verified, by touching the places, that his many pockets held their expected contents.

But he felt alone in a vast world. He could hear no sounds other than those produced by himself and his belongings; his footsteps and the faint noise of his salivation, the rustling of his clothes. It was such silence as, when on a still frosty morning a man is sitting on a hillside, will make him say two audible words only to hear his own voice, and be sure that he has not become suddenly deaf.

He was on the Oxford road, going eastward; and he had just come up from Burford by the slanting way. He had lunched there and looked about; in fact, when he was startled, he was repeating to himself with amusement a quotation upon the Cary monument: 'And plenteousness in their palaces'. It had suddenly struck him that the road was just faintly different. The part surfaced for wheel traffic was narrower; the rest, great breadth, was grassy gallops. And the telegraph posts were absent. He shuddered with misery.

Dream? Nonsensical question. No one asks it in a dream. One hundred times nonsensical. He moved to the grass; and, looking at the flowering plants, named them: betony, lady's bedstraw, fennel.

He took a few steps towards the hedge: and then he heard a note, sweet and prolonged, as of a flute. He stood still and it stopped. He took another step or two & the instrument spoke again, at an harmonic interval. He stopped and went on; and always with the same result. Someone he could not see was observing his movements minutely. With all his attention absorbed by the experience, but not in any way unpleasantly, he walked on; until at an instant there were in his legs innumerable points of pain. He tottered and fell. He had been well peppered. His last controlled thought was that the metaphor was good. The sweat stood all over him; he just waited, smarting dreadfully.

A slight, powerful man came towards him. This was delirium; but he had no power to deal with the question. The young man was a negro; and dressed as unexpectedly. The costume was right and logical enough; but of design, colour & materials such as he had never seen in combination.

The man spoke an unheard tongue. It was evidently short, sympathetic questions; and the voice was attractive. Mungo Park stared at him without a word and closed his eyes. With this action he relaxed all his muscles and lay like a rag. The nozzle of a flask came against his lips and he took a draught of its contents.

—Deo gratias, said he, automatically.

—Potui te gravius vulnerare, said the voice. Mungo Park sprang to a sitting posture with astonishment, relief, dignity, indignation.

—Tu me vulnerasti?

6

—Et non alius.

—Eccur?

—Nonne audisti sibillam?

—Sibilla? Quae est ista?

The young man pulled round an instrument which he had slung to him, the very form of which was a sufficient explanation. It was a cluster of shepherd's pipes attached to a windbag, a home-made looking thing, with a charm of age or handle or both about it. Bent on demonstration, he blew up the bag; and then, with delicate orange-tipped fingers, produced the harmonic sounds, but this time as a merry tune. Mungo Park felt wretched again.

—Nil timendum, said the man with a slight accent of reproof. Veni.

—Non possum ambulare.

—Age. Veni. He held out his hands and tugged Mungo Park to his feet: then he strode off as though he were alone, and his prisoner struggled after him.

There was no door to the doorway of the cabin, a heavily constructed building, the wooden elements by far too strong, and prodigally spacious as the residence of one man. It smelt inside of fields & woods. There was a couch, heavily built too, with a dark leather mattress and a neck rest.

The man pulled off his cap, which he threw on a shelf, displaying thick black hair, straight & glossy. He spread a textile rug on the mattress & smoothed it swiftly. The broad stripes of dark blue and red were to become familiar. Mungo Park willingly obeyed the invitation to stretch himself upon it.

The young man moved about, looked out, came back, sat on a stool, stood up, muttered, looked out again. Then he addressed to Park a rattle of remarks in his own tongue.

—Dic latine.

—Dixi mysterium; et iterum dico.

—Unde noscis Latinam?

7

—Est lingua sacra.

Park relapsed into wild thoughts, and groaned.

—Nil timendum, the black repeated; and passed into a room beyond, where he began a one-sided conversation, at first hesitating, then voluble, interminable. When he came back he said:

—Accersitus.

As the negro turned his back, Park walked firmly into the apartment where he had heard him go to speak, & advanced with the courage of a racked man going to be beheaded; his legs were painful. The appearance of the little room was a distraction in its strangeness. It was a small octagonal. The walls were of different hues, and rippled each at a different angle. It was finished atop by eight convergent triangles; it was like being inside a big crystal. A solid stool was structured with the floor, all one wood; and a furniture settle, or table, had on it a quantity of untidy blank paper & a metal style.

A soft note recalled his attention & there came staccato words: Ra tete ra. He returned no answer. The signal & words were repeated.

—Adsum, said he, stupidly.

—Bene; faveas. He sat down. Followed unintelligible words.

—Intellexisti?

—Minime.

—Tu quis es?

—Kentigernus Park Scoticus.

—Faveas voces custodem. He clapped his hands in answer to this request, and the negro came in and took the seat.

—Take a handful of those sheets, said he in Latin, and write down your own replies. Then he spoke in Bapama, but at a chosen pitch, facing squarely to one of the panels; and a long dialogue followed as at first.

—Now then, he said to Park, be clear and brief. What is

your name? And so, perhaps for twenty minutes, he performed the tedious office of interpreter. His fatigue and anxiety were shown in the increasing obsequiousness with which he transmitted the replies, often evidently considered most unsatisfactory, and the increasing sharpness with which he elicited them.

He smiled when the ordeal was over, and his eyes shone boyishly.

A whole set of relations and implications came in an instant to Park's mind: that integrity of many elements which at any moment of this recent period he had had no hope of recovering.

I am convalescent, was his first reflection. The signal went, & the black did all that he expected him to do. He was absent a long time; and Park now cared as little as he knew what he was answering about.

Let him, said he; I'll give that lad something to think about, and make him wiser.

The black returned without any remark or legible expression on his features. Park fixed him and asked (in English):

—What's your name?

The black hesitated and answered:

—Cuan.

It's like a dog, thought Park.

—Dic mihi, Joannes . . .

—Non licet.

—Dic tamen . . . he commanded angrily.

Cuan spoke volubly in Bapama, and would not be stopped by word or gesture. Park looked at him with patient hostility & presently said:

—Nihil metuendum. Cuan became at once, and remained, villainously silent. He was called and came back.

—Vocatus. Park hobbled with great difficulty to the speaking room and sat down.

—Ades?

—Adsum.

—Mox locuturus est Reverendissimus Dominus Thomas a Villa Gracili S.T.D. a secreto Amplitudinis suae vicarii generalis dioceseos Kottatilensis. Esne paratus? Intellexisti?

—Ita.

It is a dream, thought Park, abandoning all his hypotheses, as he heard the exceeding sweetness of the voice which paraphrased the message just received and went on:

—Salve, Domne Hospes, prospera sint tibi omnia, et aeternaliter.

Fluently, courteously, with the slowness of a cultured man, the speaker elicited a really rational account of Park's person, antecedents, present conditions and — perplexities.

—I have a certain theory about you, but you must volunteer the information.

—It is correct, said Park.

—But say it.

—I am a priest.

—Face the blue plate & stare at it. Park did so. Shapes quivered upon it and presently settled to a picture. It showed an interior like a room in a London club, as to human figures acting independently. The foreground figure was a big bust of a man in monastic dress. He was black. He put his hood off his head with a natural gesture and smiled, and the plate became blue again. Park faced the speaking plate and the voice went on:

—I was going to say goodnight: but I will make a few remarks to you which will not be recorded. You will receive your formal instructions later. First, be quite at rest in your mind. We shall certainly take charge of you. Stay where you are contentedly. You are a prisoner, but only of your own undertakings. The less you move and speak the more convenient. Do not let the fact distress you: but it is as well for you to know that you are the cause of hideous excitement throughout the world. It is through no fault of yours;

but the trouble is very great. So caute, cautissime. Treat the gamekeeper as what he is. When you see him, say to him: 'Ta'at ng'on'; it means 'Faith of a slave'; & give him your blessing. I will do the rest, if indeed anything else is required. Then send him to me. Excuse me further; for we shall be busy all night about you. Be well. The man will do all he can. Make him teach you some useful phrases of the common tongue; he is well educated. Memento memoris. Vale. Park had no time to linger on what he had heard. But he restrained his hurry and went back.

Cuan showed signs of misgiving.

—Ta'at ng'on. The poor fellow threw himself flat on his face. Benedictio Dei omnipotentis, Patris et Filii et Spiritus Sancti, descendat super te, et maneat semper, said the priest; and he knelt erect.

—Amen.

—Accersitus.

The gamekeeper sprang to his feet, blessed himself, clasped his hands at the height of his face so hard that they shook, & dashed into the speaking room. When he went his skin was slate-colour and his eyes seemed plates of flat dull copper: but he came back looking as usual & morally, if not quite, restored. He had his hand before his mouth as though by force to keep his words inside it, and the thought expressed by his upturned eyes was laughably transparent: Thank God I have not spoken a word. Park had to restrain himself not to feel like a sultan.

Cuan helped this unconsciously by the swift silence with which he passed and repassed, innumerably busy. He noticed his guest's fagged look: and brought officiously just the portfolio stand the Parks have seen in all ages. But the portfolio which he placed upon it!

The plates were metal, perhaps zinc, polished in different degrees according to the design, large enough for life-size heads, which was in fact their subject. The drawing was incised in thick, masterly lines; and laid in the spaces were coloured surfaces, well within the drawing; these were enamel, inlaid metal and pieces of shell, put there by pressure, fusion or setting as the substance might require. Hair in the portraits was treated as in good Gothic sculpture, & such accidents as moles, rather frequent, and scars, more rare, were evidently much valued by the designers.

All the portraits were of men; and all the horses (for horses there were) were stallions. Park had never mastered the horse; but he could see well enough that the creatures represented had been marvellously trained; or, what was the same thing, were so admitted to friendship with their masters that they knew of themselves how to stand for portraiture; and could speak if they chose. They might indeed by some miracle have become fully domesticated like the sheep-dog.

Dogs; what brutes these were; they were horrible; mastiffs, bloodhounds, bull-dogs were regimental emblems in comparison. Park thought he would come back to them later & turned all the dog plates.

At the next he almost gave a cry; pure David Jones. It was a scene of hunt animals at all planes & angles; no bother about scale; little wild horses and big ibexes, cheetahs and gazelles with their natural characters superbly emphasized.

Cuan showed his face. He saw that he was not called; but he came on, persuasively. He had changed his clothes and had nothing but a cotton tunic, breech-cloth and white sandals.

As though he were a nurse he lifted Park as he was, & carried him to a bath. There he stripped him and togaed him up in a sheet of the red and blue stripe; but not before he had looked with compassion at the miserable state of his legs, so swollen and discoloured where the saltpetre, or whatever it was, had damaged them. He touched the skin delicately, and sighed.

He went away and presently was hard at it in the speaking room. He came back with compressed lips; he laid Park on a table, made him easy with towels; and then, with a lye he had prepared, did him all over and mopped him half dry. He oiled him until he smelt like a herbarium, artistically sponging off the drops where they formed; then in a jolly wooden bowl as big as a wastepaper basket he made another lye, which, applied, turned the ointment to soap.

With grimaces and gestures he expressed: You must try to walk down into the water; for you are so slippery that I should let you fall.

He went down first to arrange the sunk furniture; on this he made his bather comfortable with his face just above the surface of the water.

Lying without sensation in the tepid bath he watched Cuan, who, besides, was taking trouble that all his movements should be closely inspected, separating and assembling all the things which had been on his body and would never be there again. He could see that it was a sort of mausoleum rite which was being performed; that somewhere in the then world there must be a museum vault waiting for its prey. He saw in his own suit and other clothes, in his purse, watch, map, tobacco, handkerchief, rosary, pencil, knife, scapular medal, keys, the pathos of stiffened clouts and trays of venerable rubbish often seen behind glass. He noted the absence of his hat and stick; and had the strange illusion that they were at x leagues and y years of distance, irretrievable.

Cuan built all to a rectangular shape which satisfied him; and then fetched a copper box with a flange lid. He examined the inside & invited Park to do the same. He laid all the belongings in it, adding only a bullet of what was nothing but camphor. So there's trade with the Philippine Islands, thought Park.

He came out of the water; was dried & wrapped in the striped sheet.

Cuan looked most foolishly like a woman handling clothes & household fittings wisely; he had the queer gestures of testing the transparency of a towel; impatient hurtling of a cloth round & round as though to discover its cardinal points; firm choice of one rather than the other of two indistinguishable objects.

He wiped and dried the shampooing table and draped it with a cloth. He placed the pile of clothing, looking shop-new, and stood attentive. Park watched and Cuan waited.

At length almost inaudibly:

—Benedicite. And Park blessed the clothes.

With reverence & tenderness, and yet with servile authority, for the ritual was a mixture of vesting a bishop and dressing a baby, he touched Park with each garment, & deftly wound it, or hung and disposed it, as its use demanded.

Park thought of the priests of the old law as he made mental notes for dressing himself in the future.

The dress felt togalike, and as if the last miracle would be that it stayed on. It was not however quite complete. Cuan bandaged his feet with a dark green scarf, prepared like a puttee. It left the toes free, turned the heel dexterously, and stopped with a tuck. Shoes over this.

Then Cuan was crestfallen. He saw that the buskins could not be worn. Park had the vanity to be sorry, for they were of white-enamelled leather, decorated with a green line.

Then came a broad woven belt passed through the fold of a half-pendant of this toga behind to the front. It had five tails at each end to make a fastening. The general effect of what the servant did with these ten tails was to plait them; but this is a gross description. Speaking generally of his residence in Ia, and the resemblances and differences which struck Park in making the comparisons forced upon him by

14

his experiences, while certain objects, like baskets, barrels, cheeses, showed a stability which nothing could upset, there were principles which seemed unfathomable; among them, fastenings. Park, after long observation and practice, after frequent and humiliating tuition, learnt a few for use; but, wherever he went, his imbecility in this particular weighed upon him; exposing him to the witticisms of Dlar, and the respectful staring of many.

Last a collar was laid round his neck. It passed under a pocket of the garment left by skilful draping, which Cuan drew over his head in a hood.

Attached to the collar was a superb medal which, from its appearance, & especially the fine workmanship, Park took to be gold. It must have been four inches across. It represented the Deipara. Owing to the intricate folds of her draperies, there must have been a thousand different surfaces, all of which were treated separately with enamel. Round about was an inscription in Roman characters – & strangely Park thought this the most astonishing novelty.

He made out at a glance: INVENTA SUM ERGO DEIPARA IMMACULATA.

Recognizing the most entrancing of anagrams, I am mad all right, he reflected; but he smiled with resignation.

Park's custom, from the seminary at least, had been to take the food set before him; and as to liquor, though he liked it, he was satisfied if there was what he considered harmony between the beaker and its contents; and asked no more:

> What–if the wine impart a golden tinge
> To thought–what skills the colour of the wine?*

When his meal was finished, taken at the couch where he had first reclined, Cuan stood before him as though waiting

---

*'Pash zezel tiffem', says the Wapama proverb: the darkest wine illuminates.

for a signal; Park wondered how he knew the time so accurately. There was a tremor in everything and then a hush as though the earth had stopped breathing.

—Hora precum, said the man, though all things said the same. Park, thinking he heard him say 'Jube, Domne, benedicere', went on with Sunday compline, in which Cuan joined.

Preparation for the night consisted chiefly of making Park comfortable where he lay. Cuan asked him if he wished to see the stars; and drew away the ceiling, showing a blue parallelogram of sky, which flooded his consciousness with an ocean of longing & regret, and at the same time soothed it unutterably. I do not speculate, Park with emphasis resolved, upon this world, its age or its human government. Certain things show signs of security; but I deduce nothing. But if tomorrow . . . He found himself already beginning to form wishes and velleities, and cut the process short.

Tomorrow! It has either gone or will never be; detestable point of imaginary time.

At an age when nights are often broken, and if a man has had the wisdom to make the best of that condition, he may feel in the morning benefit as though each of his forty sleeps had been effective sleep; and should he relish his dreams, queer or evil, he has, before the magical night has faded into the day of real pains and dangerous responsibilities, a few minutes' sense of enrichment. Park stared at the stars from his couch. He knew, so feeble was his astronomy, that it would have to be Cassiopeia or Ursa major, or some part of those constellations for him to have any pleasure of recognition. No. He wished obstinately that a particular star should be the pole-star.

In which case . . . he started ratiocinating . . .

He slept a minute; for the stars had moved only a diameter, or 'twenty four hours & a minute', said he; and slept again. The stars appear to have a circular motion; &

the pole-star . . . & he slept again. No, he was wide & wild awake, and fetched a horrible curve in stellar space. He became loosened from his couch which took a curve of its own.

I shall never be back in time, he groaned. I shall never be back in time. Every thought has two meanings. If not back in time, in what shall I be back? Shall I ever be back? 'Ever' is a property of time, & I shall never be back in time. Every thought has multiple meanings. I shall never be back in time. So he shut his eyes, and when he opened them he was back.

Yes, but am I back in time? What was that about the two kinds of time? I know. Cuan; the stars.

He could hear the voice of Cuan in the speaking room; but whether impatient or obsequious he could not make out.

Then he heard the man's voice near him; speaking in a piteous whisper:

—Dormis, Domne? ignosce mihi. Tristitia affectus, somno fractus, nescio quid amplius. Da mihi mandatum ut dormiam . . .

—Habes mandatum. And he himself went to sleep; sleep, as it were, & no more nonsense. The vision he had had, as pleasing & reassuring as it was surprising, upon the eggshell-blue plate in the speaking room furnished the nucleus of his fancies. He thought that he was lying on his face in grass, and that it was Thursday, and that on Thursday people were black. He woke and smiled. It wasn't Thursday; it was the Assumption and a Wednesday; therefore people are as usual.

His clothes and coverings were strange.

Oh, aye, said he; better asleep; and he slept.

He was in Westminster Cathedral and it was also a railway station of intolerable vastness & silence. A church has chairs, vaulting; these provided abominations on the floor and overhead. A station has taxicabs, advertisements, kiosks, angles. What a wilderness of these features. There was a covered lorry with a stupid bill pasted on its hood: 'G.S.R. Man is omnivorous'. The lorry became multiplied to infinity in dreary perspective, the alignment perfect like an army-train or a boy's drawing. Park went down the line in his vestments looking for the sacristy and a third-class smoking compartment. He had lost his server and his railway porter. I shall recognize him, for he is black. An unending train went through, pouring out passengers without stopping; all were negroes.

Park halted and addressed himself prophetically:

Go through the swinging glass doors; no one will notice you, as you are black. With a wrench and a struggle he came to himself.

That is a strange thing, he thought; to dream a fact I did not know awake. I am black.

It was light; he was chilly, for he had perspired copiously; his chin & neck were soaked. There were horses outside; he could hear the clink through the open ceiling.

In some way he divined that the horses were for himself, and he experienced one of those miserable minutes all must have known. He remembered with dread the lively expressions of the horses he had looked at in the portfolio of engravings; and at the same time that the state of his legs would prevent his attempting to ride. With rage he sprang from the couch, and his legs were well. He had common thoughts of bathing and shaving.

Cuan came in carrying a great cloak and a helmet. He spoke some fossil sentence, some 'good morning' or other; & Park repeated a syllable or two as he heard them. Evidently a start was intended.

He made to put on his shoes. Cuan did it for him, and laced them. He walked towards one of the panels of the room; the man slid it open and he passed out of doors. He could not see the horses, but there was Cotswold, earth & sky; the familiar golden soil and cool green, the coloured

18

pattern of fields, crop, stubble, grazing, early ploughing; hedges of quick, draped with clematis and tangled with black bryony. The eastern sky was a dense formation of thin, horizontal clouds. Cuan pulled and straightened his clothes, and laid the great cloak on his shoulders, clasping it at the neck. He handed him the helmet, dull black papier mâché with a badge painted on the front. There were pendant chains as straps. Cuan just tied them, a 'single knot'; the chain held. Then he took up all the back folds of the wide cloak, dropped it half and half over his two shoulders and led the way. The cloak which Cuan wore was draped in the same way, with the odd effect; and held so by a loop at the tail fastened to a button at the neck. The horses turned their heads to stare at the two men.

Cuan held the stirrup and Park mounted. When he saw what Cuan did, he threw the folds of his cloak off his shoulders, so that it enveloped himself and part of the horse. He required in fact no riding freedom: the mount was practically a pack-horse, and responsive to the least wish of the rider.

They rode in a southerly direction, so that Park expected to go near Eastleach, but checked himself remembering his resolve. They took the fields straight on, for the hedges were filled with gaps. He saw horses grazing, but neither sheep nor cattle. He distinguished houses from farms.

Dwelling houses were highly characterized, long, low, vast, with very broad eaves and a fancy shown for balconies and circular windows. He found later that the lighting was principally top-lighting, & in public buildings concealed lighting. But the farms, with modifications easily imagined, and what seemed to Park a note of splendour, were typical farms: with barns, sheds, pens; paddocks and orchards, abundant evidence of the invisible farmer's wife in the rabble of poultry; & flower gardens barricaded like a king's park.

They came to a road and took the right.

—Hot, hot, said the groom. The horses came abreast &
trotted. Park felt exhilarated.

—Quomodo vocatur equus?

—Tsup.

—Equi?

—Bini vocantur Zup; plurimi Ssup.

—Equitare?

—Tsuba, zuba, ssuppa, juxta placitum.

They rode a stream; the horses galloped, seeing their
destination ahead.

IT WAS A BUILDING in its way arrestingly sumptuous: a
two-stage rotunda with a flattened dome, all of stonework,
laboriously dressed and masoned, designed with consummate art. At a handsome distance from its base was a
circuit of low wall with many gate openings. The whole
stood in a splendid area of well-kept grass, and there were
no paths visible. Round the upper and smaller stage of the
building ran an inscription course. From the portion ex-
posed to his view Park reconstructed the words of the
psalm: Laudate pueri Dominum, laudate nomen Domini.
There were a few men sitting on the coping, dressed in what
could only have been liveries. They rose to their feet in
silence as the horsemen rode into the enclosed space.

The groom led the horses away & Park followed Cuan
through one of the circular doorways into a foyer. A servant
took their cloaks, helmets & whips, and glanced to see if
they had spurs or weapons.

By different doorways in the inner wall Park and his man
entered the rotunda.

It was a relief to Park to recognize that he was in a sacred
building. He felt his reason was being saved. Kneeling men
moved sufficiently for his accommodation. He knelt, blessed himself, and spoke to God as a man does.

His desire was to be as little distracted as possible, but he soon detected that men in choir, certainly below some-where, and probably at a prodigious depth, were singing None.

It was approaching the prayer. He heard the great clang of a bell, & the sound of a subterranean sea, as somewhere a multitude rustled together. A choir pealed, whence he could not determine: Ecce sacerdos magnus.

He rose to his feet: and could then see over the rather broad parapet where his arms had rested. He was one of many occupying a hung gallery at the spring of a cupola; it was just as it were a circular pew, for one row of men, with its seat & kneeler. The cupola leaped from the summit of another much greater and far down in the earth; & that again was supported by piers. A part of the ultimate floor at a still greater depth was brightly illuminated. This was the sanctuary; for the procession of the mass moved towards it. It was cut by the unbroken ascending line of some great element of the building and in another direction by a traverse as austere. He could see the bishop at the faldstool however; his ministers moving in ample space, and with utmost solemnity & precision, as they vested him.

This was all, at the distance, which could edify or gratify him, until two deacons passed the chasuble over the bishop's head, and Park was certain, beyond any contradiction, that it was close-sewn with diamonds.

The mass proceeded exactly as anyone can verify any-where, raised however to the scale to which the reader of this relation has grown accustomed. It ended with the publication of an indulgence in the sacred language (as the Wapami call Latin) and the vulgar tongue; and this afforded Park's first opportunity of hearing Bapama spoken with some deliberation. It made no impression upon him; he tried without success to catch the equivalent expression of a hundred days. One feature had struck his imagination: all had knelt for the credo, & tens of thousands, at any rate, had united in singing it.

Park had made a curious observation at the mass. He was sure the bishop was white: for the prelate had distinctly raised his face as he sat at the faldistorium; and, though he would not admit it to himself, he believed that it was in his own direction.

As the three rode away, he could not keep the subject out of his mind, and he addressed to Cuan many remarks tinged by this curiosity.

At last the man said, frowning slightly, and low, as if scandalized:

—My lord observed that the bishop is a pale man?

—Yes.

—God is no respecter of persons. It is not an uncommon thing (changing the subject as quickly and thoroughly as he could) on a great feast to breakfast at a club.

—You are my guide.

—My lord would agree not to make friends or even to speak?

—Yes.

—And to leave the club at the first signal from me: ng'on n'tha (I am only a servant).

—Yes. What is the dedication of that church?

—The martyrs of Uganda.

—Benedictus Deus.

—Amen. Yonder is the club.

Park looked in the direction of Cuan's whip; and laughed with pleasure and amusement as they drew near, at the extraordinary mass of horses and gorgeously dressed men.

His pleasure however was soon clouded; for his appearance created a stir, which the utmost politeness of the gamekeepers and stableboys (for such they all were) could not disguise. Many moved to surround Cuan, but he shook them off.

He made for a fat black and spoke to him aggrievedly.

The giant smiled and patted Cuan on the shoulder; but he led the way, and in quick time Park was reclining on a prepared couch and left to his thoughts. These would have been dismal had not the nimblest smiling black he could have imagined bustled up with a tray which he thrust into Park's hands without ceremony.

Instantly he splayed the feet of a folding tripod he had under his arm, snatched the tray, planted it on the stand and stood grinning. It was evident from his expression that he was supposed to be amusingly got up. Park smiled and the boy went away pleased.

He, at any rate, hasn't heard of the man-in-the-moon, he thought gloomily. But the breakfast was good. It was a delicate fry of some sort of liver, on a big thin barley biscuit, a bowl of salted water, and an orange. He had hardly finished his meal when Cuan appeared ready for riding and spoke a sentence in Bapama in which Park was proud to recognize the word ssup.

What a relief to be gone. Oh, the glory of the unchangeable sky, the gladness of the grass, the restorative view of hawkweed, scabious, calamint; the row of elms; and an addition, in Park's eye not at all unacceptable, of grey poplar, the fancy of a local proprietor, perhaps; for the disposition indicated planting; the ash, too, appeared abundant.

The line they took was as straight as they chose, for there was no standing crop in the way; and there were passages innumerable in the hedges.

There was at home a parcel for Park; a copper box, namely; and lying on it, his first mail: a meticulously folded note. It was from Monsignor Villa Gracil; & the writing was microscopic, artistically disposed on the sheet. Beside the compliments d'usage, its purport was – for it was easy & fraternal: I send some odds and ends. Have patience; I have so little. Speak to me p.m. I am called in familiar conversation Svillig. Park made an experiment in trying to think Wapama. He means to express, he surmised, that he is frightfully busy and is impatient to see me; and also that I

23

am to hold on until 'they' have made up their minds about me.

In the order of spiritual and intellectual value the contents of the box were: a breviary for the week (from which it appeared that today was Saturday); a crucifix of mature design in which (so naturally) the divine Victim was of negro type; a grammar of Bapama, in the Bapami language and character; a Bapamu-Latin (and vice versa) dictionary; a book of views in a kind of lithography; a map of Great Britain; abundance of handmade paper, a block of Chinese ink, a few brushes and four reed pens.

Once his emotions under control, Park unfolded the map. He looked for the place where he supposed himself to be; & at the point found a red dot. It was Svillig's doing; for here and there were translations into Latin, in his hand-writing, of the unintelligible words engraved. The country in which the dot appeared was called Regio principis Ednae. Kottatil, on both sides of the Severn estuary, was marked: urbs nostra. London was in the Hertfordshire direction and called Ito. The whole of Devon & Cornwall was forest; &, so far as the map showed – for a word crossed it firmly in heavy characters which Svillig had translated conclusa – quite uninhabited. The whole, saving these explanations, was one bewilderment of straight lines, rag-ged forms and unknown signs.

Park stared at it all sadly: but brightened when he saw in the minute script, somewhere about Lincolnshire, the words Villa gracilis indicating a small property.

As he folded the map Cuan came in & he asked him the time. The man pointed to a horizontal scale on which an indicator was moving clock-wise to the right. The bar had six great divisions, which equalled together a third of the solar day. When the indicator reached its course, it ran back with a distinctive murmur, not to zero, but to the first of the strokes representing the smallest subdivision (for it took just the time of one 'second' to run). The result was that, when the indicator stood midway on the scale, the time was (in our horology) noon, eight in the evening, or four in the morning. At the moment it wanted about a division to noon.*

Park worked a long hour extracting from the dictionary a Bapama-English vocabulary; with frequent questioning of Cuan when he was present.

For Cuan was busily doing housework. He had a subordinate whom he kept out of sight, perhaps to spare Park the mortification of seeing a pale man in a menial position. Cuan did not mean too much by it when he said ng'on n'tha.

At noon he told Cuan to call Monsignor Villa.

With the most charming mixture of politeness & familiarity the speaker talked over with Park the events of the day, the contents of the box, the beauty of the season, the miseries of life.

—You were at the high mass at the martyrs?

—Is the martyrs a big church as churches go?

—Well, yes. Did you recognize the assistant priest? I saw you; but I have uncommon eyesight.

—Much, if not quite all, is very strange to me.

—Tell me, Drak, have you everything you wish?

—No. Park heard him laugh.

—Of course not. Is there anything we can do for you?

—You mean relatively small things?

—Yes.

—Well, Svillig, I need to be shaved.

—Ah, precisely; that is a point. We want you to grow a beard. Please do not be grieved.

—I am sorry.

—We shall try to make it up to you for that and other

*This is one example of the discord between Wapama numeration and that which prevails in the world in the twentieth century. Its intricacies will be shunned in this relation, and precision often sacrificed to a general intelligibility. The Wapami use the week of seven days and lunar months. Spare days are dies non and extra festivals.

inevitable sorrows. How old are you?

—59.

—Ah.

—My beard will be grey if only with age.

—Ah.

—What did you say?

—Are your parents living? Park could not answer.

—Drak, I am an imbecile. I would come to see you, but the order is strict.

—Do get permission and come.

—You are to come here at the earliest possible moment. A condition is that you know quite a good deal of Bapami. I will try to send you a tutor. Stare at the blue plate.

The vision was not Svillig, but an old man with infinite wrinkles on his kind face, and a tiny fluff of white hair. Park showed his surprise; and from the expression on the plate he knew that the vision was mutual. The old man made a casual gesture of benediction and disappeared.

—The vicar-general, said Svillig. Vale.

No ONE could wish Park to recall the miseries of weeks which followed. The tutor soon appeared. He was a religious, & aged. He had the ways of a Cistercian. His principal business remained prayer, God reward him; & his pupil profited by his example in this particular. His duty of tutoring Park he seemed to regard as a species of agriculture or forestry. Whenever the pupil attempted a distraction he would resume with vigour and authority: Pay attention to the passive; it is most irregular; and perhaps for that reason little used by the uneducated. Or:

Mind the dual of this noun; it is very peculiar. Or:

Quick, stir your brains, give me the accusatives; look alive: gaping nostrils, odd ears (wrong, get it right), bandy legs (come on), short stilts, an unequal marriage, blind twins, ugly brother and sister, quarrel between friends, blue eyes, a one-legged man.

26

On All Souls' day – & he detected some dim allusion to release from purgatory in the selection of this for his first introduction to men at large – he went to a great cemetery where Svillig, whom he had often seen surreptitiously, introduced him to a multitude of people.

At sundown began a booming bell. All stood uncovered, reciting, inter se, the De profundis with incredible slowness. The psalm and the bell stopped simultaneously.

—There is a foundation near here, said Svillig, where, by special and ancient indult, mass for the dead is said continuously; do you grasp my meaning?

—I think so.

—And nobody knows (except, of course, a cobweb of erudition like you) why.

—It drives me nearly mad ... Park was beginning. Svillig hated reminiscences; and always detected them before they were born.

—It doesn't matter, said he.

—Yes it does, answered Park.

—It does not, he rejoined; for all pale men are on the verge of madness; & (as you would say) discourse is wasted on certainties; and he laughed his irresistible laugh.

—Come along, said he; there's a jolly supper, goslings and cider.

—I say, where do we stay tonight?

—That's good too; we're staying with a doctor.

—What of?

—Medicine, he said, with a look of feigned innocence. I won't say who it is, as I should like you to get a shock.

—I don't know one doctor from another.

—You soon will.

27

THERE WAS nothing but a gentleman of scientific eminence in Koti Ra; every sign of perfect breeding and new acquaintance marked his welcome.

—I have for some reason, Drak, said he, been appointed president of this commission.

Svillig seemed sometimes to have a power of moving the pupils of his eyes, and did it now.

Koti addressed his two guests, now both, now one, now the other.

—I have thought of different places; perhaps you will advise me. It had better I think be on the surface; not so convenient perhaps, but desirable.

Svillig was assenting.

—The Dominican convent has a good chapter room; it's frightfully inconvenient, but the speaking room adjoins it. We shall have to rig up a lot of furniture; for there's only one seat and that's all round the wall; and A Ra himself is not allowed to sit in the prior's stall. They have a private descent; but it's always out of order. They might be glad to have it put in repair.

Svillig gave a huge laugh, and it infected the other two.

—I thought, he went prosing on, that, if we started the examination at once, it might suggest to our distinguished subject an impression of informality in what we do, and rather screen from his notice the strictly scientific aims of the commission and the oppressive stringency of the commands under which we are acting.

—Do you mean . . . Svillig began.

—Yes, I have asked two of my colleagues. We could do a bit of examination. You could make notes for the protocol. You are a physician, aren't you? Afterwards we could all have a pleasant evening.

Drak by temperament could hardly put out his tongue or bare his arm for vaccination. But he started to strip, &, as no one forbade him, he continued. He was introduced naked to the two other doctors.

They measured, examined and pulled him about for an hour, making only their own observations to one another. Then one of them handed him one of his garments, and he dressed slowly, out of suppressed irritation, while they whispered together.

—Capital patient, said Koti Ra. Park perceived his good intention of apology and dropped his bad temper.

—We were wondering at your athletic and beautifully proportioned body. You have taken good care of yourself. You have only lost four teeth.

The old man took one of his hands, looking at it like a connoisseur, verifying its thinness and firmness and the position of the thumb.

—Finger nails on the small side, he remarked. How old are you?

Park determined to be courageous, & answered: 59 (in Latin; as Bapami knows no such numeral). Horrible silence.

—Gentlemen, said Koti Ra authoritatively; 59 what?

—Solar years. Renewed silence. Koti Ra compressed his lips and asked:

—And how many days?

Park calculated and answered:

—245. That is, he added, in decimal numeration.

He thought it possible that it was in order to relax tension that Koti Ra asked with polite curiosity:

—Decimal numeration? You used that?

—Yes.

—I wonder what could have been the origin of that. (Svillig was turning over the leaves of a book.) Come; let's have supper; and talk merrily like five old friends.

THE SERVICE was in no way in excess of the meal: bird broth; candied and pickled fruit and vegetables; and the expected goslings, tasting of lemon. There was great variety of biscuits; the wines were sweet and not strong; and there were delicate morsels of cheese looking like wooden matches, taken at any time during the meal. At the end there were fine peaches; and sweets which no one took.

When, as has been said in certain times and places, the cloth was withdrawn, for there was never any sign of any cloth, Koti said:

—There are several reasons why we cannot address questions to the most honoured present, & doubtless his wisdom has divined what they are. But nothing prevents his asking questions of us. Talk at table is sacred talk.

So Park began:

—There is the surface population of this island. Is it denser in other parts than in this part?

—Its density varies exactly with the productivity of the soil.

—The soil feeds the whole population?

—Yes, and it is the greatest thing done in Ia.

—The moors and hills are uninhabited, said another speaker; except by wild creatures.

—What?

—Different kinds with antlers, including the great kinds.

—Wild swine and bears.

—Hunting forests?

—Yes.

—Who use them?

—The nobles.

—How are they hunted?

—Mostly with dogs.

—What's the name of that long-legged feline?

Svillig looked pleased and said: N'ti. Have you seen it?

—Yes, in captivity.

—In captivity?

—Yes, & often in pictures. I saw it in a picture the first day I was here, on the eve of the Assumption.

—Did you though?

—So this surface population consists of nobles, cultivators, & noblemen's servants?

—You can express it still more simply; as the noblemen are the cultivators.

—Have I exhausted your patience?

—Not at all.

—The subterranean population.

—What about them?

—Are they numerous?

They looked at one another in bewilderment, but one said:

—Yes.

—What's their origin, race? Is it all one?

—Oh, you know, that is a terribly hard question.

—There are scholars who bother about it.

—Who will certainly come pestering you whenever they get the chance.

—I approve of that sort of investigation, said Park. But I am only seeking the most general description.

—That would be, said Koti Ra, that their race, or races, and origins are not ours.

—Conquered, you know, said Svillig sadly. Poor people. They must have had a bitter handling at some time; eh, Koti?

—Oh, yes.

—Have you seen any? he asked Park.

—No. Do they ever come up?

—Practically, no.

—What prevents them?

—No force of law or prohibition. They are obliged to come up, for example, on professional business; sometimes by medical order; for certain journeys . . .

—Military exercises, Park put in. At once he experienced the odd feeling of twenty-to or twenty-past of his former life. The four men pretended not to have heard the remark.

—I think Drak means, said Koti, voluntary ascents.

31

—Yes, that was my idea.

—They are very rare, but not impossible.

—Why, in one word, do they stay down?

—In one word, said Svillig, because they like it.

—Subject to the law of God and the church there is complete freedom for all.

Park fetched his breath, and said:

—The natural law, the positive law, the ecclesiastical law . . .

—Is the law of the empire.

—Before which there can be no inequality.

—What is the form of government?

—Representative.

Koti Ra saw that the conversation would become interminable, and rose.

He led the way to Drak's rooms, looked round, touched this and that, adjusted a light shade with a host's magnificent servility, and went away in silence.

After a time someone came through the door and passed round the screen; it was Svillig. When he saw how Drak was engaged he himself knelt down and remained so until he had finished.

—Koti hopes you will be comfortable. All your personal belongings have been brought to this room, said he, walking towards it.

Drak stared.

—Yes, he said, you will be here for some time. Here's the speaking room. If you are called it will be the night secretary. Ah, there he goes.

—Ha, said Drak, meaning 'attentive'.

Svillig could hear that it was an enquiry from a stranger, an embarrassing enquiry, and he perceived that in fact Drak was embarrassed.

—I should tell him, he said, to deal with all correspondence till morning.

Drak gave this direction; & Svillig, speaking at the

resonant pitch, added: discretion, infinite discretion.

Ng'on n'tha, said the secretary.

—Tomorrow, said Svillig, you will be provided with a chancery; we are putting a lawyer in charge of it.

—Are you on the commission?

—Rather. I am the canonist.

Park became unutterably sad; & felt as though he would never speak again. Two men came in with a loaded tray. When they had gone Svillig poured out a sip of some cordial and Park drank it.

—There's a lighter side to everything, said Svillig. I am going to bring you a fellow called Dlar. I cannot say much about him; for he is in a peculiar legal position; he has been under more than one cloud. He is a charming companion, and he knows many things. He is inclined to be saucy. But, whatever he says or does, he is always a black man; and as true as the almanac.

—Don't go away.

—Drak, remember every human being is unique; & the duration of time is best regarded as one second.

—You mean: Cheer up and go to bed?

—Something like that.

DLAR walked in alone. He said bluntly, as he handed a folded note: I am never announced or accompanied (he meant by a servant).

Drak made a conventional reply and unfolded the note carefully. In contrast with its intricate creasing it contained only one word, the size of a gnat: Dlar.

—We have a friend in common, he said.

—Svillig is so much to me that any friend of his is my friend.

Dlar was a beautiful man. He bore a strong resemblance to Svillig, apart from the colour of their hair. This against black skin looked almost coral. In Dlar it was browner but,

33

if possible, more extraordinary; for his skin was no darker than swarthy. The type, however, was pure enough. He wore a small beard.

He rattled on, to promote acquaintance rapidly. Then, fixing Drak with his great white eyes, he said:

—Speak always to me as plainly as you like; otherwise, he added with a smile, I shall have an unfair advantage of you.

—It is like that, is it?

—No one, said he, is allowed to speak ill of me; the law protects me. I see, he said, that I puzzle you. I am one of the dead. It is a fiction; I am reckoned to be dead.

Drak had it on his tongue to make a whimsical remark, but refrained. Dlar spoke in great earnest:

—I have been condemned to death and reprieved.

Drak leaned forward.

—I am in consequence regarded in many ways as though I had suffered the penalty I deserved. I am deprived of most of my civil and ecclesiastical rights; and also of many conveniences. I may not hunt, or have men-servants, or publish books. I cannot be a witness or a judge, or bring an action, or exercise a profession. But, on the other hand, no one may touch me either physically or morally: no one may sue me or send me samples or prospectuses, or ask of me alms or other favours; or, as I said, speak ill of me.

—There must be some strange psychological consequences.

—But I may do as much good as I like; not, however, adopt anyone; and say what I like about myself, with moderation.

—Dlar, Drak exclaimed.

—I am expected not to boast, however judiciously; &, in general, recommended by my confessor, my relations and friends, indeed by the whole spirit of our nation, to try to behave in all ways as though I were dead, only awaiting the judgment. Can I do anything for you?

34

—Yes, you can, said Drak with sudden resolution. Hear my confidences, if I can ever get them uttered, and comment on them as ruthlessly as you threaten in fun.

—There is no fun in me that I know of. But let me make a start.

—Willingly.

—Stop that nonsense about being only 60.

—How do you mean?

—Let others estimate your age, Koti Ra, or me, or anybody.

—What good would it do?

—Say you are 300.

—How can I?

—You have been asleep; you have used some horrible drug. Say Yes.

—No.

—You have been in the empire of Belial.

—I cannot understand.

—You are a priest.

—I am; but how do you know?

—We are all recognizable.

—So I understand.

—You were a missionary.

—No, I am a professor.

—What of?

—Moral.

—Have you seen the vicar-general?

—On the blue plate, yes.

—He is a relative of Svillig. He has also been very good to me.

—What relation is he to Svillig?

—Let me see. You know what a great grandfather is?

—Yes.

—Well, he's the great grandfather of Svillig's great grandfather. Dlar laughed cruelly. I told you you have been asleep. You're not awake yet, I must be going.

—When are you coming back?

—Soon and often.

Koti Ra came in.

—Dlar, said he, if you saw anyone who could trot along to the Dominican convent and introduce Drak to the prior, would you do your best?

—I was going in that direction.

—Good, said the Ra. Perhaps Drak would ask his reverence to expect me about noon.

THE BUILDING with its cloisters covered ten acres.

—A vast old convent, the prior said, proudly and apologetically. It has a subterranean church, but we have been cut off from it; & it is now a vicariate. We have a surface church for the office.

He led the way to it. It was entirely stone-built, very heavy, severe and vaulted. In style it was clearly linked with the churches of 'antiquity' thought Drak, using the word in his mind for the first time. The cloister was older, vast, spacious. By way of ornamentation it was designed so that there were no longitudinal lines but those of the plan, while the vertical lines were as numerous as could be, producing an uncommon effect in the perspective. He dreaded to mention the chapterhouse & did not see it. The solid walls of the cloister had been built true enough to be a surface for painting, and had in fact been painted in some past time; but now only vestiges remained.

There were wooden seats in the windows & they sat down.

—You have known Dominicans?

—Many and well.

—Distinguished?

—Yes.

—Any named Thomas?

Drak thought and answered:

36

—Yes, I think only one.

—Not . . .

Drak caught an expression so wistful on the prior's face that it saddened him.

—Alas, Father, he said, I was born far too late: but I know well what he looked like.

—From portraits? Was he not very stout?

—Yes.

—Did you ever know a master-general?

—Yes; two.

—What were their names?

—Andreas Fruehwirth and Hyacinth Cormier. Drak saw that the surnames were Chinese to the prior.

Dlar approached and said:

—We must not forget the message with which Koti has honoured us. He hopes to be with your reverence about noon.

The prior excused himself and walked away.

—That is a most peculiar thing, said Drak, chiefly to himself.

—What?

—The habit.

—Is it changed?

—No, said he, except for the bare feet.

—This lay-brother, Dlar whispered, wishes to hear you speak your own language. Dlar introduced him to the brother.

He smiled and addressed him slowly and cautiously:

—Is it Inglis?

—Yes.

—You say.

Drak said with the utmost distinctness:

—Good morning, brother, I am glad to see you. I hope you are well.

Brother Mark struggled with his vocal organs; and then, with a comical gesture of discouragement, said in Bapama:

—Say a few words to me in the classical tongue.

Drak thought and said:

—My tongue is the pen of a ready writer.

—Calamus velociter scribentis, brother Mark almost shouted with joy, irradiating the countenances of the other two men with his happiness.

It was a day off for Drak. The two friends left their horses & walked in the direction of Koti Ra's house by way of the river. The contrast between the scene and his companion was so poignant that Park had again & again to renew his resolution to abandon himself to his present experiences without reflection. He would have liked to make a confidence of this; but by no means could he find any way to express his thought. As they walked for the third time through the water of a shallow, well-built ford he said:

—No bridges?

—No, said Dlar, we only use them on the fast traffic roads. I sometimes think, said he, that it is one example of a sort of harmless hostility we have towards the subject race. You never see them walk in water.

—Then how do they get about?

—They don't. And that is not all they dislike; in the same way they hate the upper air; and they cannot endure the natural light of the sun.

—Whatever took them underground? Were they forced?

—In a way it must have been that; and yet not entirely. Let's get some food here.

They had entered a paved yard as though to cross it, when Dlar made this suggestion.

—Who's the proprietor?

—I forget his name if ever I knew it. He's a fanciful kind of chap, often underground. Mixed blood; artist; there's something odd about him.

The host was black enough and a gentleman, but he

could not conceal his uneasiness quite.

The greetings & hospitality were chiefly in facial express-ion and disconnected syllables.

They were taking the simple meal, an egg thing, some-thing like an omelette, some dried figs and raisins; beer, and the invariable cheese.

—The children, said Dlar. The man said:

—The elder is not quite well: and the little one is shy.

—I told you, said Dlar, that there is something wanting. No black man behaves like that. You know what the truth is: fear of our beards.

Drak made no answer and Dlar seemed to relent.

—I do many bad things, said he; I must make it up to him. Just help. Put on all your villainy and hypocrisy.

Drak was jolted by this, but decided to laugh too.

—You're not dead, you know; though he thinks you are.

—There is a sad want, said he, when the man re-appeared, in this delicious repast; that our host is not seated with us in conversation. I, Dlar, have the honour to present Drak, Koti Ra's guest; a stranger among us.

—Ini'in, said the man, greets you, sir, and desires to welcome you often.

—Drak, said Dlar, wishes to know why, he means the profound reason, why underground folk are where they are. If you cannot satisfy him, nobody can.

—May I fetch a cool drink?

When Ini'in came with the wine, he had the host look and manner which beautifies all men. He stood still. Dlar with his natural clairvoyance said:

—What if we took the wine out of doors?

They passed into an enclosed quadrangle as beautiful as a bowling green, though the elements of its beauty were simpler: a sheet of peerless grass, with an enormous stone astronomical object in the middle; the grey wall, a triumph of proportion. A table was ready set under an awning; on it were three cups, a bowl of peaches, an empty bowl for refuse and an earthenware cradle for the wine-bottle. The sky, blue and white.

—I admire that jar, said Drak.

Well he might. For it was spherical with a short small neck.

—It has a name, said Ini'in; showing, in barbaric incision, made when the clay was soft, the word: Esperu.

When the wine had been tasted, Ini'in said:

—It is certain that the underground tunnels and caverns are in part more ancient than our coming to this island. They are excavated & strengthened with consummate engineering art; & are still the wonder of our greatest men. It is even supposed by some that these works were carried out by people of whom no other record has remained.

—People almost mythical?

—Yes. For if, it is said, you place them anywhere in history as we teach it, you are faced by an intolerable paradox: mechanical construction & genius we cannot overpraise, with moral degeneration the most complete. The palace of Vulcan inhabited by rats; Vulcan & the rats contemporary, if not identical.

—Well?

—Why, to make a short ending of a long story, when their troubles came upon them, they took refuge underground and are there to this day.

—Contented? asked Drak.

—I think so, said Dlar and Ini'in at once.

The two children came and had a look at the visitors.

PERHAPS it was the wine speaking; or more likely human and cultured intercourse had stropped his wits. Drak spoke, or thought he spoke, with intelligence, as they walked home to Kota, and Dlar was laughingly benevolent.

—Dlar, said he; is it right to ask questions; first, in general; specially, of dead men; most specially, here and now?

—Yes, yesser, yessest.

—I think I see what protects the questioned.

—What is it?

—The crystalline truth of the answers he might return.

Dlar stood off, faced him; &, staring like a trunkless head, said:

—Drak, your skin is white, more's the pity; but you are black inside. Ask questions.

—Are you on the commission?

—How could I be either judge or witness?

—No, I remember. Have you any instructions from Koti Ra?

—Yes, though not explicit.

—Thank you.

—Svillig spoke plainly enough, Dlar went on; you know, he & I are very great friends; we are related – though of course everybody is, unless they are tainted. We were educated together; and besides, he added, meekly and with emotion, I am his dead man; for he was my advocate at the trial.

—Trial?

—Yes.

—You were tried?

—You should think little of your own annoyances, great and grave as I know they are.

—I see your drift.

—Yes, I am coming to it. Svillig said to me: Kentigern Park (Dlar pronounced the name, in spite of its awkward consonants, without fault) is a friend of mine & I wish you to shield him with the whole of your ability. That was all, and that was enough.

—You know English? said Drak in English.

—I do, he answered, in the same language; but, he added in Bapama, never mind that now.

—And Koti, he continued, means that I should go about

41

with you, answer your questions and bring you to the sessions in as good a temper as possible. You are an irritable devil.

—I know; but consider my age.

—I do, said he, with a meaning grimace.

Park was swept off his balance by the alertness of this man's mind, and the swiftness and accuracy of his judgment.

—Now that you have heard the confession of a conspirator, said he, listen to the advice of a friend; everywhere in all this ghastly enquiry coming on, always say what you think. Afterwards too, even to the highest. What you think is generally known beforehand.

—I expect my thoughts are engineered for me.

—Isn't that so always in intelligent conversation?

—In debates, no doubt.

—And nothing so delights a cultivated mind as to be surprised.

—Hazardous procedure, Drak murmured.

—It eliminates fools. It eliminated me.

—Will those sessions be public?

—Most of them.

—Will pale people be present?

—Certain. For millions of them are scientific people. But watch old Koti. Only observe the seat of the commission. The convent has no vehicular access. It is enclosed; no woman but an archprincess can enter, and there is no archprincess; for A Ra is in sacred orders. The weather will be wet; there might even be snow.

—How are pale men treated?

—The question answers itself each time. Some of them are highly intelligent, some not. But, in general, remember that as a guest of the oligarchs you rank with them; & know as little of the others as you did of the barbarians of your own time.

—What's the order now? he asked; for they were back.

42

—Hulloa, exclaimed Dlar, there's a sentry. Excuse me. The order? Let me see. A big bath; vespers; assembly; supper; pleasant evening.

Drak's servant met him.

—David desires to wait upon you. Will you see him before the bath or after?

—After.

David was the man in charge of Drak's temporary office. When he came in, he uttered the compliments in one long hyphened sentence; and continued, without pausing:

—The correspondence has been heavy. It will soon be registered. We are getting two more clerks. I have here an analysis. Shall I read it?

—Do.

—There is nothing at all involving risks; although there are numerous notices and citations. Drak looked up.

—Nothing, nothing at all, he said, and went on.

—There have been 600 calls, all dealt with; nothing significant; except:

One from the archprince (herewith the message & the answer returned); fifteen from the Mgr Villa (all abandoned); one from Cuan Niger, head gamekeeper to His Highness Prince Edni: I have found geranium pratense; we killed three salmon. There are 155 letters from learned societies; sixteen from newspapers; four from theatres; a selection acknowledged. About a thousand uneducated letters. Publications not opened. Instructions?

—Docket the society & newspaper letters, & submit them.

David had foreseen this request: & handed the packet at once.

—Pick me out a few of the miscellaneous letters; and six newspapers, illustrated. The lawyer withdrew.

EDNI RA was a stately old man. His dress spoke itself old-fashioned. He had a military bearing, if there was such

43

a thing; and, if so, not without cause. Wapami thought and speech dwelt little on genealogy; but no one could hear the name & not remember the general whose genius was a landmark in history.

To what was still reckoned one of the greatest names was linked the finest property in the island. It corresponded roughly with Park's former summer playground, Cotswold. It contained therefore all the sources of the Esi, and the Ra had peculiar rights over the river until it reached the municipal boundaries of Ito. He raised important crops; and the Edni herds were celebrated though not numerous. The pride of the man, qualified by his simplicity, was, for one reason and another, admired. 'As black as Edni' meant the perfection of breeding.

Edni's estate was, in Drak's eyes, the summit of culti-vated beauty. There was not an eye-sorrow upon it. The Camp, as the residence was called, was a string of palaces stretching for five miles along the edge of the bluff overlook-ing the valley of Kottatil. Forming roots, as it were, to this terrific dwelling, was an escarpment such, that the view of the Camp from below was as astonishing in another way as the prospect from its terraces and countless balconies.

A touch may be added to this summary description. There was a very great yard where Drak easily located the village of Birdlip; and from it shot eastward a stretched-string road such as the Romans would have envied. It continued so until it joined the circular road upon which Park had been hit. Some former Edni had not only brought this route to the straight, but with great labour had levelled it. It was a princely causeway, flagged all the way; and very carefully kept, as some knew; but so skilfully as to appear almost neglected.

A drive with Edni Ra from the Camp to his villa was marked by Edni simplicity. A couple of scouts rode half a mile ahead, & were of course always in view. The driver was motionless: for the horses knew what they had to do & there was nothing to prevent them from doing it. The group of overseers rode far enough behind for their clattering not to be heard. And the old prince drank in the vision all the way.

The houses of the villa stood on an eminence which seemed artificial.

One day Edni Ra remarked upon it to Drak.

—There is an ancient town under this.

—Yes, he said.

—You say Yes, said the Prince. Do you know its name?

—Cirencester or simply Ciren.

—Say it again. Drak did so.

—I wonder, he said slowly. I have heard the ploughmen call the villa Sirri.

In the big hall of Koti Ra's house Edni Ra came towards Drak the moment he entered.

—Our visitor, Prince, said Koti Ra.

—What's his name?

—We call him Drak; but he calls himself by other names.
Edni Ra looked still attentive and expectant; so Drak said:

—Mungo Park.

—Is that just a name?

—Yes.

—Has it any meaning beside being your name?

—Mungo was the name of a saint.

—I never heard of that saint.

—And Park as it happens means in my language an enclosed property.

—Does it though? Changing the subject he said:

—We are acquainted in a way, aren't we?
Drak smiled.

—I say, Koti: I want to be a witness in the enquiry or whatever it is.

Koti Ra beamed inexpressible satisfaction. Drak noticed stenographers hard at work.

—You know, said Edni, on the very day of that most unfortunate assault by my gamekeeper I had posted a guard of fifty men all along the north boundary of Edni, with orders to take a description of every stranger. I was abroad when I got the unhappy news. I started home at once; and I communicated with that incomparable Svillig. Ah, there he is. Villa, come and listen.

—Through that competent channel – that was you, Villa – we made shift somehow.

—Drak was an admirable guest, said Villa; weren't you, Drak?

—I am very grateful to His Highness.

—You were surprised by the shot?

—I was surprised before that.

And so on, at length and in breadth.

When Koti said suddenly: Prince, will you sup? & the dozen or so of men moved in one direction, it flashed upon Drak that another informal session of the commission had taken place; that he had been turned inside out, and every fibre of his mind explored.

He sighed and wondered where Dlar was. The thought of the dead man evoked his image and expression of valiant cynicism. Drak stiffened his spirit, and flung himself into enjoyment of the repast and the wild banter of conversation under the rose.

It may or may not have been the next day – it might have been even a month later.

The days, wonderfully varied in persons & particulars, were standardized by an irreducible fact: Drak was a prisoner and a tormented prisoner. He thought often of Herman Melville's Three Years in the Marquesas Islands; and another, a Russian book: Nine Years Captivity. . .

He lived holding on to his courage, and sometimes to his reason, with a death-grip. But the screw was tightening, the rack lengthening.

Yet, so he consoled himself, life was never such life before. He had the support of religion. He heard mass daily at home; for Kota, like all great mansions, had a private cupola similar to that to which he had ridden on the 15th August. He made his confession regularly and said his breviary. He rode daily; he could be as abstemious as he chose; his bath was restorative; and, strange to say, he never dreamed at all.

He paid one free visit, by Koti's express permission, to the prior of the Carthusians.

Well, on this day, Dlar walked in with his sunny impudence.

—Though you are sixty you need not look like Methusaleh.

—It is a horrible sight, I suppose; what do I do?

—Do? Why, get it cut.

He saw Dlar intended elaborate teasing and resolved to outwit him. He called his servant; and, when the man came in, he could not remember the word for a hairdresser. Dlar with downcast eyes looked his most mischievous. Drak said to his servant the word 'coiffeur'. The servant went away as though he had understood.

Both men laughed.

Drak told Dlar the story of the man with the little head and the big beard. Dlar liked it, and repeated parts of it, correcting the diction.

—You told that story better than usual.

Drak looked up as someone came in. It was David. He brought a copy of the newspaper Eon and pointed to a paragraph.

THE EDNI SHOOTING CASE

This morning Cuan Niger, gamekeeper, appeared in magistrate's court no. 25 and answered the interrogatories. The man was ordered by the magistrates not to leave the island without their permission.

—Do you make any comment? asked Drak.
—I will write a few notes, said David.
Drak handed the paper to Dlar, who looked at it and returned it in silence. Dlar read his friend's thoughts and said:
—Never defend the accused, unless you are employed to do so. And let David do his own work. Have you seen this?
Drak gulped down his misery as he had often to do; and took the small volume Dlar held in his hand.
From old habit he looked into it for faults; yet, though his eye caught them everywhere, he was charmed by the type & the disposition of everything.
—Do you detect any errors? Dlar asked.
It cost him one of his greatest efforts; but so anxious was he for Dlar's good opinion, that he said:
—Yes.
—You will point them out to me when you have time?
—Willingly.
—It's not published, you know; I am not allowed to publish books.
It was a collection of short texts in English, mostly inscriptions; but many, by what unheard-of miracle, must have survived through manuscript or printed documents.
Drak was sunk in such a prodigious dream that, for the first time, he paid no heed to what Dlar was saying. He recovered with a wrench, and asked:
—May I have it for a day?

THE PUBLIC sessions of the commission had begun. Fatiguing as it was for Drak, he recognized Koti's kind wisdom in arranging the informal meetings. For, as witness after witness was examined, a sworn report was passed round in print to the members and formed the basis of the questions asked and statements made.

Whenever the president looked towards Drak he rose & made a statement, which usually had been carefully prepared with Dlar's assistance. David was always present; and often diverted the session by his influence, though his voice was never heard.

Perhaps the commission had in reality fulfilled its mandate, when there was a sensation. Drak had come to have almost one mind with his dead friend; for he was detached & cynical as he had never expected to be. He guessed, correctly, that the 'sensation' had been, if not exactly pre-arranged, foreseen. The Registrar announced in toneless words that the late Dom Egid Reni of Reni, S.T.M., D.C.L. . . . This was Dlar. He never reached the end of the sentence; for five commissioners spoke at once, and were presently joined by others. Disorder became such that, after a few minutes, Koti rose; and the grooms ran for the horses.

Next day the chapter room was crammed; the cloister was dense with reporters. The inspector of police sat in the speaking room talking the whole time to his subordinates.

Koti said the prayer Actiones nostras. It was just silence before the storm, which soon broke and rose and raged. Before long it was understood that Koti had said: The session is private. He remained standing; and this, with the arrival of twenty-five policemen, brought quiet and then dead silence. Koti ordered the stenographers and David to withdraw; and sent away his own clerks.

—Be seated, gentlemen, he said. The date and place of the next session will be made known. There will be no record kept of what I am about to say. I suggest that we complete the labour of the present session walking about; & that will afford anyone who desires it the opportunity of apologizing to Dom Monaco Parek!

What urbanity there was. What a thunderstorm rolled from the blue sky. At last the prior craved permission to enter. After a word with Koti he announced:

—As I have obtained from his lordship the bishop dispensation from silence & abstinence, I am able to offer you, gentlemen, some simple hospitality and do so.

The hope was whispered about that Dlar might be present at the collation; and, in the refectory, there he was. Each sat where he chose. In every direction two men were looking persuasively for Drak to sit between them. Dlar said to him:

—I will tell you about it; such fun.

Svillig said to him:

—There will be a banquet this evening.

—Where?

—It is not known; it will be left to ballot.

Svillig & Dlar were in Drak's room, talking with excitement which they took not the slightest trouble to conceal. David came in, & joined in the conversation almost as an equal. He said:

—The correspondence is horrible.

All laughed.

—Take a week to it, said Drak.

—Make it six months, said David. There are however a few things.

—Any risks?

—None that I know of. And (in a whisper) I won't bother you about the gamekeeper.

—All right. Anything else?

—The archprince is confined to bed.

—You returned the correct answer of course?

One of the dreadful pauses followed which made Drak's heart stop. The two Wapame saw that David was the more to be pitied; for it was he, a trained lawyer, who had brought out Drak's unfortunate words.

—David, said Dlar, you're no pea. You're a melon.

He seemed grateful for this gross familiarity.

—Away with your business, continued the dead man; get on to the rumours.

—There's one more item of business, said the lawyer lamentably.

—Shall I deal with it? asked Svillig. He took the paper, & read: Her Highness the Princess I commands the attendance of Koti Ra's visitor this day week; simple dress.

—Answer, continued Svillig without hiatus, the subject bows to the earth.

Drak, in his anguish, remembered what his physician had once said to him: When a man is going to die he does it.

He jettisoned all his fears and miseries, and said to Svillig:

—Many thanks.

Koti came in. He beamed expressively on Drak, who tried to express in a look all his relief and gratitude, and was understood by the old physician prince.

Svillig and Dlar remained looking at Koti Ra in silence; for they knew he had something to impart.

—We had better tell Drak the news. You are enfranchised and ennobled.

Drak wished he were either awake or dead.

—When all I want, he reflected bitterly, is a pair of tacketty boots, forty pounds a quarter and a miserable life.

The three men interpreted his expression with great accuracy.

—You have yet to experience freedom of movement in Ia; it is a good land, said Dlar.

—In a sense the whole island will be your own and you will have a particular property, Svillig added. Have you heard (to Koti) where it is to be?

—It's the old place called Trouble Farm; but the name is to be changed. Mention it, Dlar, for it was your suggestion; & you can pronounce the word.

—Park, said he.

Damn the grandeur, muttered Park of Park to himself.

—Trouble Farm, said Svillig, belonged to Edni.

—That's right, said Koti Ra. The archprince has allowed him to relinquish it.

—What handsome thoughts black men have, said Park.

Koti thought the tension was enough and became boyish.

—Come now, guess where the banquet is to be?

—Here, said Park.

—Right. And who's to be here? besides ourselves? (glancing at Dlar).

—Well, the members of the commission.

—Of course. And old Dr Eza; you liked him.

—And Edni Ra?

—Yes. The archprince is ill; but he is sending his nephew, Toni Ra; he's quite young. And eleven more.*

—Speeches? asked Drak.

—They are printed and handed round. If any are spoken, they are limited to about 20 words.

Svillig caught Drak's eye and said:

—After Toni Ra you will rise; and, looking towards him, say: I remember all your Highness's kinsmen and all the faithful departed. Not one word more. All, except Dlar, will stand for a moment. You sit when all sit.

When he came out of his bath Park found a complete set of new garments laid out for him. They were striped like his old blue and red (which was Prince Edni's livery); but of colours which really charmed his taste; ash-colour & a very dim rose. His shoes were of the latter colour, as also the foot bandages. His girdle and collar were of cloth of silver. No ornament was hung on the hook of the latter.

In the drawing room he was presented to Toni Ra; who looked like an undergraduate, as he was. He wore the royal livery, white; and he had a sky-blue cap.

His friends had so fully primed Park that the banquet came near to unqualified joy. But as the misery hung over him until it was burst, Koti said to him, with an unbeliev-

*Meaning, of course, 8.

52

able want of formality:

—Get it over, eh?

Park nodded.

Koti rose and sat again.

Prince Toni rose and said:

—Sir, the sovereign, my august uncle, regrets his absence. He commands me to offer, & you to accept, a token of his princely benevolence.

Park waited until an equerry brought him the object, glanced at it, and, rising, pronounced the appointed words. All happened as predicted. When the medal came back to him, for it journeyed round the company for admiration, he saw that it represented a sailing ship, white on a blue and green ground, and that the reverse consisted of the words, in sumptuous lettering, DORMIO, SED COR MEUM VIGILAT. Koti hung the medal on the empty hook; & everybody smiled. The evening was most lively; and the young prince stayed so late that when he left the party broke up.

Svillig left reluctantly at the end of the third watch. Tedious as it was, he had to journey down to Kottatil, where he expected to find business fiercely accumulated, as he had been so much absent.

Dlar, who took little notice of day or night, or where he lodged, continued the talk which had principally occupied the three friends: on setting up the new establishment, and the future management of the little estate. The dead man was willing to talk to exhaustion, for the sake of the parentheses which every now and then he would contrive to include in the conversation; as for example:

Yes, I approve of that, stick to the tradition.

Nothing changed; no, not the colour of a cartwheel.

Quite so; formation of a library.

Edni will be most loyal; he will keep out of the way. He will seem not to interfere with you.

Yes, call on Edni often; once a week. Always go when he

asks you. Always show yourself on the blue plate whenever you have been speaking to him.

These & innumerable counsels were carried out as Park's life drifted gradually to Park and at last came to rest there. He learned the ways of proprietorship and hospitality. He used a convenient cupola for his daily mass. It looked into the Carthusian church. Occasionally he went there for the night office. He fitted up an oratory with Prince Edni's advice and assistance. He used his library for a division of every day, & began systematic study of the Wapami classics. Usually in the company of the Prince, he ranged far and wide over Edni; & sometimes, though rarely, beyond it.

IT WOULD not be necessary, even if it were possible, to produce a very lengthy summary of the documents bearing upon his legal status which, with no great delay, were delivered to Park. The barest will, and must, suffice.

There were two written documents, which might be called the Patent and the Title; two printed volumes named respectively the Tenure of Property, the Oath of the Nobility. Add to these, before Park could hope to understand them, comments of the faithful and magnanimous Dlar.

The friend spent much of his time at Park; & Drak was often a guest at Reni, the delicious villa in a hollow in the chalk towards the high down. Many hours of the day and night were spent over the matter.

It became a black man, said Dlar, to understand his position as fully and clearly as he could; and, he added, in his character of a friend, he might be awkwardly caught if he did not.

Very roughly, then:

In the name of the Father and of the Son and of the Holy Ghost. Amen. Considering the divine clemency, inscrutable, has bestowed upon me, A, hereditary prince and vassal of his lordship the Emperor, who for the present purpose shall be no further described, the charge of a gentleman hitherto unknown to me personally, I have, in council, considered it opportune to appoint him a name, Kentigern Park, together with rank and property suited to his origin, learning, ability and merit, which last I believe to be exceptional.

Before all, I direct him to call to mind at least once a day the end for which he was created, and to submit in all matters which concern his salvation, and the conduct of this present life, to his ecclesiastical lord, the archbishop of Kottatil, and to continue in constant and sincere communication with His Grace at least indirectly.

The property now called Park was to be his unto long years, meaning until he reached the age of 400, when a special edict would permit, that is, force, him to retire to Kano. He was for ever exempt from burdens fiscal, parliamentary and administrative. No one may cite him, sue him, ask favours of him or speak ill of him.

And let no one, however exalted, presume to surmise that these exemptions are in any way connected with any fault in my beloved subject for which he could be answerable to the law. And if anyone, in malice, or jest, or even in the good faith of ignorance, should express such a surmise, he is to be sharply corrected by the nearest justice.

Park had to administer his property well, disposing of his produce as directed at great length.

Though for health and recreation he might take 'feather and scale' under existing restrictions, he was to abstain from any exhibition of horsemanship and from great hunting.

He had access to every library not the property of one person, and to all museums, but not laboratories, at all times except from matins of Holy Thursday to the second vespers of Easter Day.

He had complete liberty throughout the island, though access to the forests might be denied him; & beyond it in the provinces specified, and over all the great ocean & the long sea; always keeping out of sight of Kano the continent, unless unavoidably driven thither. Nor was he to possess any map or plan of the continent, its rivers, lakes, ports, harbours, docks, canals, cities, railways, mines, and so on exhaustively.

—No one will provoke you to mention Kano or think of it; and you should let good example guide you.

—With respect, why is the permission to journey not general?

—Because many places, islands especially, but great continental tracts as well, are in practice inaccessible.

—For example?

—Well, the great peninsula is all forest, timber, mines, some quarries, hunting. The cornland is only corn and industrial fishing. There are very great experimental areas. And again many provinces are governed with difficulty; and may be, for all I know, under martial law, or something like that.

Drak was going to say something.

—Stay, said Dlar. I will answer you what is in your mind. It is as well for you to know what no one ever mentions. There is the military establishment for the empire. I have no military rank; neither have you.

—I understand and thank you. What about the islands?

—Why, can't you guess? Don't you remember how you scored off old Eza during the commission?

—No.

—He said you were born in Hindi.

—Yes, now I remember.

—He pointed to a little island in the southern ocean, and asked how you escaped from it.

—So he did.

—You told him you had webbed feet and walked home.

—Shockingly rude. But I was tormented and everybody was laughing.

—Well, we send to the islands people who are wanting other things besides webbed feet. The mad, for example, and people who cannot take care of themselves or their property; those who are a danger to others, from a variety of causes; those who cannot be corrected of practices we hate, like making money out of sport.

—Beside out-and-out criminals.

—Yes, many are penal places. All those classes are far more numerous than you think. For remember it is a big empire, & its populations are in many places dense, the races are heterogeneous, & in all stages of racial decrepitude. Ia is misleading; its people are extraordinarily docile to good government. They have ability of all kinds, mechanical, scientific, artistic, and are in consequence very well off.

—You interest me.

—We must find you opportunities of verifying these facts. Our province is more like a happy family than experience would lead one to expect. In that view it is a pattern to the empire.

—And in others?

—In others too, though less important, if not negligible, it has a lead. Its industrial arts are in some sections unrivalled, printing for example and the related arts, illustration, engraving, bookbinding, calligraphy. Its pottery is said to be unsurpassed, even by antiquity. I daresay you judge well of the common things we use daily. Smith's work again. There are sixty gates* of which I say no more; with their sixty names, which I am not privileged to repeat; and they came out of the forges of Ia, the island where I was born, my Ia.

While he is not absolutely forbidden to pass beyond the frontiers of the empire and enter the regions at present

*Meaning 42.

occupied by infidels, he is cautioned, even though he should take such a journey in order to carry the faith of Christ to those who are without knowledge, or being inspired with the thirst of martyrdom, not to be unprovided with all permissions, the usefulness of which is self-evident; but he is forbidden to trade in those regions under any pretext or disguise; and he is recommended to consult with men of known ability, for the better understanding of this prohibition.

—They will tell you, Dlar volunteered, if they are honest, that the blackest man, being au fond the white rat that he is, is liable to go sneaking about, dressed up in pagan clothes, riding on pagan camels, violating pagans' graves, digging up pagan ruins, not for the love . . .

He looked at Drak and saw how round his eyes had become.

—Don't mind, Drak, there will be some consolation for you when I have finished; but you must learn.

—Go on with what you were saying.

—. . . not for the love of tablets and sculptures, of vessels and paintings; not for the love of history and antiquities; not for the love of knowledge, but for the love of loot & vainglory.

—Nevertheless . . .

—(as you rightly say) if a man is so primed with knowledge, so chastened by meditation, that he expects to find no more in any place he may visit than what he takes with him, then he may go into deserts, look reverently upon what is to be seen, and having seen it come back on foot and empty-handed, to continue his classes or his meditations.

—The region of the infidels is the same place as the empire of Belial I have heard you and others mention?

—It is usually called by that name.

—Where is it?

—You should infer that, with your good knowledge of geography, from what we have often said together. It

58

consists of not quite half of the land and water surface of the globe.

—It lies round the . . .

—the what?

—We called it, said Drak, the 'Pacific Ocean'.

The name & the fact must have struck the mind of Dlar with sudden and exhilarating force.

He almost shone with pleasure and scorn. 'Pacific Ocean', he repeated in every tone, laughing loudly and bitterly.

—Called also the swamp of iniquity, the marsh of ineptitude, the lake of fire, Pacific Ocean, Pacific Ocean.

—You like the name?

—Drak, he said softly, may I just speak to Oli of Han'na? But you don't know him?

—No.

—May I, while I am speaking to him, ask him in your name to come to Park?

—Do so, indeed.

—You will like him.

—Is he dead?

—Not yet, said Dlar; and went into the speaking room.

He came back.

—Delighted!

—Good, said Drak.

—Will you come and speak to him?

—With pleasure.

The usual palaver.

—Speak English, Dlar suddenly interjected in a tone of banter.

There came a slow quavering sentence:

—I am much honoured by your invitation to Park.

—Most welcome, said Drak.

Dlar manipulated the blue plate. Drak, as the image appeared, uncovered and smiled; and the image disappeared.

The dead men walked back in silence to the study, staring at one another like conspirators. Dlar spoke:

—Services to the state, unrewardable services.

Oli was a white; of a most repulsive type.

ONE MORNING of mid-December there was a call from Svillig.

—There's something. Have you time to slip down?

—Yes.

—You are sure? No engagements?

—None.

—Anything tomorrow?

—Nothing; all is clear.

—Then ride to Bisli Public Descent. Train to Kottatil 65 Lower. I will send a clerk to meet you.

—Right. I start now.

When the lift came to rest it was evident that the attendant had sent some signal, for the stationmaster was there, obsequious.

Park had never been underground; he struggled as with a nightmare.

Let things happen, he upbraided himself; you cannot control them; no reflections; do what you are doing.

Though he had only fifty yards to go, and the coach was waiting, he felt relief when at last he reached it through a whirl of impressions.

—All as desired? asked the stationmaster.

—All.

—Any message to Monsignor Villa?

—Park of Park has started.

—In good health?

—In good health.

He opened his novel, and went on reading it. When the train stopped he showed not the slightest interest in anything. Nightmare faces appeared by hundreds. At one of the stops the door slid and someone said:

—Kottatil 65 Lower. N'gon n'tha.

He looked at the man & thought it was still the Bisli stationmaster; but the innumerable other people looked so too. A rough way was thrust for him through the crowd; & presently he was met by the ecclesiastic. He was black, thank God. But he would have walked through fire to Svillig.

—Is all well? asked his friend.

—Perfectly.

—You look tired.

—Well, I am that; but never mind.

—I mustn't delay to show you the thing, as you have come down so amiably.

He produced a full-size careful drawing of a carved inscription.

—Do you see what it is?

—Clearly. It is a bit confused: but I have no doubt it can be put straight. It's a smashed epitaph.

—It is that, isn't it? he said proudly.

—Undoubtedly.

—Now, what do you say? Could you bear to come along to Villa Gracil? It's a long way, but there's a very fast train running for some hunting people. I have managed to secure a coach; & if we have a companion or two you are sure to like them.

Park showed elation. Svillig added:

—We shall get some food on the way; and we go through Sul.

As they walked down the steps to the vestibule of the vicariate, Svillig showed dismay.

—We shall need assistance, he groaned, to force a way through that crowd.

He looked over his shoulder and gave an order to someone:

—Four porters, armed. And they waited, having no choice.

Park's thoughts were he knew not what. There was the vision before his mind of a struggle such as no dream had ever shown. But his acquired black blood stood to attention, calm.

The dreadful type of the crowd, showing no variety that he could distinguish, fascinated him. The eyes were large and prominent, looking to right and left, rabbit style; noses were hooked and thin, teeth prominent. Rodents, thought he; and all know what a relief it is to find a definition.

Four men appeared, looking like gladiators with their metal helmets, body armour & greaves. Their arms were bare. At their belts appeared the ribbed hilts of their weapons.

The crowd gradually opened a passage for a few yards; then it closed again, helpless through its own pressure.

The men shoved with energy; at last to no purpose. The whole group were presently enclosed, in apparent danger of being crushed. When the men had breathed:

—Once more, said Svillig; and at it they went.

—Ola, ola, shouted Svillig; may a gentleman not walk to his coach, though accompanied by a churchman of rank? Are black men so treated? Are dead men so treated? (For Park at the time was dead.)

This was the climax. With piteous horror all who heard tried to be somewhere else and shoved with the guards.

—You'll have to draw, said Svillig. Out flashed the weapons. To Park's unutterable relief they were 'only' whips. There were screams, the crowd climbed upon one another in terror.

There then began shouting, lashing, screaming somewhere near at hand; and the crowd broke.

Svillig smiled; but he was as near white as his colour permitted.

—I'll give him something, he muttered. Park was grieved

to hear for the first time threats uttered by that gentle voice.

There was no missing the way to the coach; a corridor of people led to it. The two entered it & stood there. Svillig had just control of himself, but looked savage. The stationmaster appeared. Where were the railway people? Svillig soliloquized; where were the police? What clerk took my instructions? Not a seat; not a fan; not an attendant; not a cup of water.

—Take a message for the minister. Take a message for the chief of police.

—Reverence, he pleaded; a slave, a slave. Dead nobleman, an orphan slave.

—Behave, said Svillig. Where are the cases?

—At Sul, said he; & at Sul there is a coach with dining room and lounge; and doubled attendants. The station and the bathing pool will be cleared.

—Excellent arrangements, said Svillig.

The stationmaster disappeared like an image from the blue plate.

—What a way to say the itinerarium, said Svillig; and smiled. Hold on till Sul, he added; it's only five minutes.

And here they were at Sul.

—Come on, it's glorious; the water is boiling hot. How long? he asked.

—Twenty minutes; no hurry.

—Stick everything in.

—Everything. N'gon n'tha.

Little by little, what with the hot plunge, the lick of fragrant oil, applied and wiped off by accomplished men, clothes newly ironed, the odd and happy meal in the train, the harmony of all things was restored; whether it was the hunting passengers coming into the lounge from idleness & curiosity, or crowds of inquisitive rodents, staring, everything seemed as it should be. At the destination, there were the necessary horses and a cart for the luggage. The farm-manager, who drove the cart himself in a simplified country way, brought with him a little black spaniel, named Sufi, which almost wept with joy at the sight of Svillig; though she knew well whom to expect, for the farm-manager had told her fifty times.

They started for Villa, trotting along the surface of the road in total darkness.

—We are passing on the right the Cathedral of Eli. It has parts of a very old building, they say fabulously old. You may know something about it.

Drak thought he was fainting.

—Did she stumble? asked Svillig.

—No, said Drak.

—Here we have to take to the grass; I'll ride in front, whistling.

He rode on, singing Decora lux.

But the horses knew the way and they arrived at a gallop, clattering into the yard.

Svillig was a happy host. He rarely saw his old, lovely home; a very great farmhouse. The massive interior showed huge beam members of the building; and the floors were enormous flags. A mighty fire blazed. Much of the furniture was part of the structure: the big table; the settles built to the walls. There were heavy screens, painted with Ia work.

The gentle little secretary, a church student, & a careful archaeologist, was sent for. He appeared as only two white eyes in the dark doorway, for he wore a monastic dress, perhaps Benedictine.

—Shall I bring the plate? he asked almost at once; for he knew what had brought Monsignor Villa to his home.

Two men carried it in on a board and placed it on the table.

—It's a fine thing, said Drak, in general appreciation of the inscription with its handsome lettering and pedantic style.

The drawing was brought.

Drak asked permission to touch the tablet; and moved

64

here & there a fragment, for the plate was smashed badly. As he made these changes, the young man marked his drawing. There were gaps, two or three only, and not large.

—The restoration will not be difficult as to the epitaph, said Drak.

—You can read it all?

—Practically, yes; I should want to think over that patch, said he, touching the biggest gap.

—Just roughly, then, give us the translation.

When he finished, Svillig said:

—That's not all.

—No, not quite.

He waited for Drak to finish and Drak would not. They became obstinate.

—That's all, Svillig said, sternly; & the young man left quickly and silently.

Silence.

—Svillig, said Drak.

Silence. Park decided to give way.

—Nothing remains but the date.

—Exactly, said Svillig.

—I have heard you speak so bitterly; and, if I may say so, so unreasonably . . .

—You are welcome to say so.

—when the subject has been chronology, that I thought I would run no further risk of provoking you.

—-I have not expressed to you all the bitterness I feel.

—I confess I am hopelessly puzzled.

—We are friends.

—I am happy to say.

—Well, what is the wretched date?

—A.D. one, seven, seven, seven.

—A.D. really means anno salutis nostrae?

—Yes. It is decimal numeration.

—Even so, the very figures are a solecism.

—Don't be angry.

—What doctor of the church was living at that date?

—I think St. Alphonsus was already born.

—At the risk of repetition, I must say to you that, upon the authority of historians the most competent, we require at this date at least ten thousand years, decimal numeration, to accommodate ascertained historical tables. Centuries of labour, flawless learning; incontrovertible conclusions.

—I am not angry; but I decline to say one word more on the subject of chronology.

—Then what are you?

Drak made no answer.

—Excuse me, Drak, I must leave you for a few minutes. When Svillig returned he made a sort of venia, and said:

—I ask pardon; and if you remember the place & circumstances, you will grant it more easily.

—Most completely, said Drak.

—Come along and see things.

Owner's pride and guest's curiosity were about equal. The difficulties of inspecting in the dark, except for carried lights, were nothing to the friends. Their shadows reared, leaned & drooped in a barn like a church. Sheds, pens, stores, buttery, larders, the bath, were visited.

The sanctuary lamp burned in the oratory, crypt-like & white-washed, with a three-quarter-circular apse and small round windows. There was a chaplain resident at Villa. Representations of angels covered the walls of the apse; and figures of Benedictine saints were on the lateral walls.

There were three rooms of greater height, one a library, and in each were many portraits produced upon the wooden walls, panels of inlay and painting.

Supper was in the old kitchen, where the fire burned. There were four: for the chaplain came and the student. There was a big, shallow pie made of pigeons and onion; & delicious beer. Drak thought he had supped; but the cook in person brought with evident pride a dish of two split pheasants and cabbage done in stock.

66

—In the country, said Svillig, we are supposed to have country appetites; a good supposition.

The rest was tropical fruits and sweetish wine.

The other two, while at table, received from Svillig (& they addressed him by that name for the time being) enough attention to make up for all possible omissions in the past, plus a considerable deposit for the future. They early got permission to retire; and the two friends settled down to a night of conversation.

A very long time passed over matters suggested by what Drak had seen going round the house; much to tell and hear of ancestors, builders, subjects of the portraits, one a martyr.

—The builder of the oratory was a Benedictine as you see by the decorations: Benedi, Scolasti, Mol, Truta, Metil. Truta is Gertrudis, whose writings nourish our devotion to the divine Heart.

—They exist?

—Do they exist!

—So many have been lost.

—Those have not been lost.

—How I wished on the fifteenth of November . . .

—On the what?

—I made a slip, and spoke in my old style. I meant the feast of Saint Gertrude.

Svillig answered Drak's thoughts as accurately as if he had heard them expressed; and seemed not to hesitate; moreover, from the periphery of the subject (namely, why the unhappy Drak had not received those faculties without which a priest feels like a being in abeyance) he pierced to the very centre of it:

—You guess, my dear friend, he said, speaking in Latin, so as to introduce the term of affection which would have sounded strange in Bapama, many have been ceaselessly employed trying to find a solution of that difficulty.

—I am sure of one.

—You remember our first conversation?

—Well.

—Every churchman who has seen you is sure of what we both know.

—Dlar once owned it.

—The vicar-general is certain.

—And the archbishop?

—Does not wish to see you.

Drak hung his head; and Svillig feared the conversation would have to break off.

—No, no, Drak, said he firmly. Great courage. We are talking only of facts, not at all of opinions.

—Yes, I understand, said he.

—For he cannot solve the difficulty; and he tries more than anybody.

—I acknowledge my ignorance.

—And we our impotence.

—So explain whatever it is right for me to know, from the rudiments.

—Well, we know you were born.

—But not when.

—Exactly. You had, and should have, a bishop.

—I can name him.

—You cannot.

—It was . . .

—Come back to the difficulty. Dare to tell me you are thousands of years old.

—Is that why I am a dead man?

—If you promise to leave that for another and probably longer conversation, I will answer 'Perhaps'. Are you thousands of years old?

—How can I be?

—How can you be? And yet uncountable intelligent men say that you must be.

—What a fix.

—You say you are 60 (decimal numeration), he said, with a charmingly malicious smile, which obliterated the last vestige of his anger. We do not believe any of your statements of the kind.

—You do not believe me? But here I am; I am in physical & mental health. I give an account of myself with its myriad particulars, which are all harmonious.

—I believe you in a desperate, syllogistic way; for you are my friend. But that you were born 114 years ago I must deny; for we have proof that you are older. That you were born in Ia, on the same wild and contradictory understanding, I absolutely deny; for we have a complete list of every birth, in its proper genealogical setting (I mean of the surface race) for the last thousand years. You would bear a certain indelible mark as well; and you are without it. I could see it at this moment if it were there; but it isn't.

—If only there had been a celebret in my pocket-book. But there was none.

—But there was none. Come now, a celebret is only a testimony; it needs supposition of the bearer's truth to have what value it has.

No good, Drak; no good.

—But surely the Curia . . .

—The Curia says: I believe the man was born; I cannot go a step further.

—But in time, said Drak, with sinking courage.

In time, barrier after barrier would be surmounted; but the last would be unscalable: admiratio, the astonishment of the laity.

—There is the whole empire.

—You know what the Carthusians said to you.

—Yes.

—I don't mean to say that I know; but when you went to see the prior I could not help guessing what your errand was; nor be mistaken in my guess.

—And you knew the answer would be just as evident?

—Most unhappily, that is true.

—What would the laity think?

—Every thought known to human folly.

ALL the pleasure part of Villa was its garden. It had not been made in Svillig's day; but neither had he been an unworthy inheritor. There was oak, grey poplar, edible chestnut.

—I like the beech, said Svillig; but I prefer it in Dlar's country.

There was a good grove of mulberry trees, growing on lawn-kept grass.

—A little contrivance, said Svillig; but nothing exotic, no cutting of hedges, no decapitation of trees; I let the willows grow.

—How right.

—But flowering-plants must be planted and replaced, selected and cultivated.

—Aconite. There was a vast spread of it.

—You mean the yellow flowering-plant? How beautiful it is. Do you like this?

—Iris reticulata.

—Iris reticulata, he kept repeating. What do you call this?

—Winter crocus.

IT WAS of no use for Drak to pretend to himself or anyone else that the command he had received from the princess I was anything but a fatigue, a torment, a drenching misery. No one would help him; and when the day and hour came he presented himself in deep wretchedness.

However, as he had so often found, the play acted itself. The stable boys might have been his own; he threw his cloak & helmet into the first hands he saw; shook himself in his clothes, drew over his hood, stroked his beard.

—Parek'n Parek.

Two bulky janitors looked like a music-hall turn. Strangely, he thought of them as negroes.

There was a carpet on the stair! At the top were heavy curtains looped up with cords.

Now I am mad. Drak was beginning to worry, in his old style.

Circular vestibule, with a circular carpet. On it a major-domo of military bearing; two servants who elsewhere would have had powdered hair.

Passages & more curtains. At last some ladies; very tall, very slight; black ladies with white complexions. Then . . . Toni.

Introductions; embarrassing for Drak, who lacked all experience of female names & titles. The ladies had each some slight defect, an uncertain consonant, a little deafness.

These blemishes might have been called 'the princess's evil'; for in the presence of their mistress the sufferers were completely healed, spoke like other people and heard distinctly.

This palace had too a vocabulary of its own. Vara Darling & Toni Boy and other such expressions were in common and frequent use.

The princess sat on a gilt stool, about which tall ladies were palely grouped. There was no pallor about her. Drak knew nothing about ladies' dress; but even he could see that the princess wore royal robes. Toni said:

—Park, Ma'am, bows at your royal feet.

The princess replied in a very beautiful voice; she observed the effect of it upon Drak.

She chose to regard her visitor as a species of wild man, not dangerous, but to be humoured; whose interpreter & exponent her nephew was. And in some strange way Toni Ra was entangled in the imbecility of his charge.

Thus:

—Toni, dear, ask man how long Ia.

71

—The princess desires to know, said Toni, how long you have been in Ia.

Drak, as though he were in the drawing room of Circe, said something of which he himself did not know the meaning.

Toni said:

—About a few years, more or less.

—Ask man how he like Ia.

—Yes, said Park, speaking out of his turn.

Toni interpreted:

He had been deeply impressed by the number and variety of his experiences.

—Has man found all well?

—He is happy at present.

No one smiled, least of all Drak.

Then the princess addressed him directly in usual Bapama:

—While they go and eat their cake, come and sit by me.

Gratefully Drak dropped on the footstool at her feet & knotted his legs into comfort.

—Good, said she.

—Your servant, Ma'am.

—Tell me now, in your country, the ladies, are they beautiful?

—Yes, Ma'am.

—They are white, aren't they?

—Yes, Ma'am.

—And beautiful?

—Yes, Ma'am.

—What do they do?

—Needlework.

—What else?

—They ride.

—Ride? What?

—Horses.

—Horses? What for?

—For pleasure.

—What pleasure?

—Hunting.

The princess I, having extracted a scandalous secret, proceeded in her own way to keep it.

—Vara, Wu, Netji, Vi, Zinta, Tu, Anavapala, On . . .

The ladies re-entered hurriedly; and in a torrent of words the princess gave them an exhaustive account of social life in another civilization.

The visit was an entire success. As he left the palace the majordomo delivered to Drak from her Highness a beautiful box composed entirely of natural sea-shells. It contained a perpetual almanack, which Drak unfortunately broke.

THERE had been long mention of a day underground.

Drak had told Dlar of his day at Villa Gracil; & though he had not specially dwelt upon the scene which took place between the vicariate and the railway station, Dlar recognized that it had made on his friend's mind a deeper impression than appeared evidently.

—There must have been, he reflected aloud, some little want of foresight, & I see the cause; but, using the prudence indicated, there is no reason to fear a recurrence; for it is a cause for fear. You are known by description to every police officer, he went on; and they have their instructions; so, even without sending a word of notice, and nothing is simpler, you are practically guaranteed generous breathing room, unless we are rash.

—As we shall not be.

—We wear our 'dreadful' beards. I do not think any superstition enters into it, but terror of dead men is general among the humbler sort. We won't take any food down there; for that would be asking for embarrassment. We might go to a club; but there would be a crowd when we left, and the police might be rough; you never know . . .

The dead men alighted at an unfrequented station. Even so, Drak thought Dlar had been over confident.

—There is a little more crowd, he remarked, divining the thought; but we shall get along.

He walked with insolent indifference as though he were on a moor.

—The type is repugnant to you, he said; but you will overcome it in a few minutes.

They turned into a broader street.

—Now, just pull yourself together, said Dlar, as they reached the end of it.

The warning was opportune; for Drak was stunned by the vision. The broadest street he could have imagined was dense from front to front. The wall opposite had lateral galleries above one another, up and up and up; all crowded. The length in either direction vanished in the perspective.

There sounded a piercing double whistle, answered & repeated until it died in the distance. They plunged into the crowd going left-ward and moved with it.

—Let's go to a book-shop, Dlar said slowly.

A great splayed opening, brilliantly illuminated by its own lamp, pointed to its apex, the entrance to the shop. Innumerable books were displayed in the immediate approaches, open and shut; just a shop window, without the window.

The shop recalled the reading-room of the British Museum, in its design and arrangement; and also in the use being made of it by readers, with clerks attending to their wants.

As they passed the barrier into the centre enclosure, the inquisitive could not bear the strain longer; heads bobbed up like those of a herd. Going there at all implied the pretension of learning; and beside, one of the two men was the notorious Reni; and the other ten thousand times notorious.

It seemed to be custom, or at least becoming, that books

should be brought and displayed upon a stand. Newness, typography, format, design; all possible properties of books were exemplified and commented by the two book-lovers.

Presently it was a portfolio of drypoint engravings. Drak exclaimed with pleasure at the sight of them.

—I know this man's work.

—I do not think it's possible, said Dlar.

—These engravings are by a man whose name I do not know.

—Coye'i the scene-painter.

—Thank you – who engraved a zinc plate.

—It was not zinc.

—Well, whatever it was, which I have seen . . .

—Pray where?

—In Cuan's hut.

—In Cuan Niger's hut? Well, perhaps yes; Edni does unaccountable deeds.

—No man other could have drawn these; except a man in my time.

Drak was silent and blushing.

—What's the matter? Do you want the portfolio?

—I do, said Drak; but it's so odd, I have not the least idea how to buy a thing.

—You just take it. 'Park, you know', he said to the clerk.

—How do you mean?

—It's charged against your crop and sales. The auditor might reject it: but in fact he will not. You could send up ten times that.

Pause. Dlar said to someone:

—Could you fetch that copy of the bound work?

In this unfolding world, stimulated to use whatever black brains he had, Park saw what was forward as the great volumes were produced: a princely present from Dlar.

For empanelled on the sides of the binding were the Park colours: diagonal bars of ash and dim rose and a round, back & front, of inlay: his badge, the sailing ship & the motto Dormio, sed cor meum vigilat. And the work itself!

It was all too precious; and he had to judge hard, to be rightly restrained in his acknowledgments. He succeeded, for Dlar said:

—See the best of all, as to the embellishment; and with that he displayed the painted inside of the boards, in glowing opus Iense, golden without the use of gold.

—Scenes from the Summa, said the giver, in reverent and delicate banter.

Such indeed were the subjects: for there may be lovely and expressive emblems of what is abstract.

—And he . . . said Dlar, looking towards a man.

Drak could only stare, as he tried to master his feelings.

The man was a rodent in whom age had emphasized the features of the race, adding all the insults time matures; who wore, most horribly, great convex amber spectacles. Drak was only aroused by Dlar calmly finishing his sentence.

—. . . is the man whose taste and knowledge composed this masterwork for the painter to execute.

Hil'nu, he said, introducing him, is a great scholar. He may tell you all he knows, but I could not do so.

Hil'nu said he was honoured, and that he was a student; but he explained all the paintings. How delightful it was; what humour and rich allusion.

—Would Hil'nu . . . Drak began.

—Too delicate, Dlar whispered; but ask him nevertheless.

THE DEAD men left the rotunda.

Dlar was reciting to himself: O res mirabilis! Manducat Dominum; and Drak finished the phrase: pauper, servus et humilis.

Drak was struck by the absence of doors in the doorways, even to a church. They entered a lighted tunnel at the end of which they found themselves in the vestibule and next in the church itself.

There was exposition. They prostrated themselves and knelt, two among a crowd of people, kneeling or standing motionless. A passage was clear right down the vast building. By the enclosure of the presbyterium they took two cloaks from a rail and put them on. Drak followed his companion round the back of the high altar into a spacious choir, where again there were many men, among them not a few ecclesiastics in surplices or rochets.

Drak knew what his business was, and tried to attend to it; but when their visit was at an end he had a clear enough idea of the monstrance and its pedestal. The latter was stone, circular in plan, increasing to the base in a gentle curve; the inspiration had been the trunk of a tree; and the pedestal at its foot melted into an ascending flight of steps, also circular in plan, but from a different centre. The whole structure covered the floor of a rounded alcove as to half its area, and the rest came forward. All the wall of this alcove was cased with small plates which seemed to be ivory. From the pedestal rose a column of natural crystal which at the desired height took the form of a four-sided receptacle, now enclosing the actual monstrance, which had been placed inside it by a door towards the alcove from the top step; above this the columnar form was resumed.

Swags and pendants of natural leaves and flowers were disposed symmetrically.

In multitude and variety were candlesticks of painted smithwork, with lighted candles, standing on the pavement of the choir.

Though with reticence, Dlar confirmed, as they left the church, that the precious materials were as supposed.

For, said he, it was right to use in worship the rare things of the creation. It would not be becoming to make use of such choice substances, nor decent to covet them, for personal ornament; and it would be futile as well; for carrion (one of his synonyms for men and women) could be sufficiently adorned with imitations of diamonds . . .

—. . . and pearls, added Drak.

—Ah, he sighed, there you name a tragedy; pearl is now only a word. What was a pearl like?

Drak was put to it to describe a pearl; but he persisted hopefully.

—Like a soaring bubble? asked Dlar.

—Yes, but dull, with a certain tenderness to the eye; some seeds suggest the appearance; they were rather heavy.

—And women wore them?

—Yes.

—Was it allowed?

—It was approved, applauded, envied. I have seen a woman with pearls tied round her waist.

—Tied like a rope?

—Perhaps not that. But the expression 'ropes of pearls' was known.

Drak thought a moment, and said:

—You mustn't think that I disapproved of ladies wearing pearls.

—What ladies?

—Those who possessed them.

—You know better now.

—I have made you sad.

—That's true.

THEY had gone out by a different passage; & on through winding, branching tunnels.

—What's the sound? asked Drak.

—No one could tell you. There are strange acoustic effects; it is evidently some industry; some punch at work; it may be at a really great distance; it's not disagreeable.

—No.

Dlar, quietly resourceful, had recalled to mind deserted passages and caverns.

78

—You may be lonely if you use a little judgment, said he.

It was a strolling ground, enclosed by its walls, without shops, dwellings, or galleries; just pillared space. Here and there was a dot of human beings. Drak no longer reacted to vastness; & all the less as a new sight arrested his attention: one end, namely, of the piazza, which was a natural cavern, pleasing by the incidence of its shadows, and fantastic in its stalactite formation. They could not but turn their steps towards it.

It was converted to pleasure, lighted enough, railed in dangerous places, provided with short runs of steps; bridges hopped the gulfs. There was a purr of water, invisible in the depths; hard to catch, however, for the rustle of little torrents. There were alcoves as it were for conversation; and a pacing length for such as might be finishing off a quarrel. They reached a circular alcove having a bench cut round it. They stood still for Drak to be astonished; for at intervals on this stone bench sat archaic figures cut in the living rock; figures at once friendly and horrible, figures which seemed to say: We are as we were made; there can be no question. They sat, powerful in their volutes of drapery, holding illegible objects with dreadful strength.

High-relieved on the roof, but carved without any structural reference to it or to one another, were two figures of angels, if they could be so called; for they bore some indication of wings. The friends were seated side by side, and looking up at them, when most unexpectedly a high-pitched resounding singing of one voice began. Both were held by it so that they remained in their then attitude. To Drak it was unearthly in its fervour and pathos, though the singer was manifestly young; & they never knew if it was boy or girl.

When they had waited in vain for the song to begin again, Drak saw his own pleasure, but not his own surprise, mirrored in the face of his friend.

—You arranged it, Drak hazarded.

—Not at all as you mean.

—You were responsible in some way.

—In some way. You like it?

—You are the author of the song.

—Did you catch the words?

—Yes, but I only remember the end:

> Lin on ti vip'thu copi thou,
> Len, len, len i'n lon.

Please repeat them to me.

—August on the downs, said Drak, when he had heard the whole poem.

They talked on, and Dlar's drift was that this trifle was in no way in the Wapama taste; but, as was perhaps discernible, he had had English models in his mind.

—I have turned it into English, said Drak presently. Will you hear it?

—Joyfully.

> Lambs are drifting up the slope
>   As in silence they feed;
> Little clouds, so still the day,
>   Seem wandering overhead.
>
> No sound on all the down
>   All the day long.
> The minstrel no one else has heard
>   Sings, sings, sings his song.

—Thank you; & the dead men repeated the version, improving it as they did so, until there was no need to write it down.

—I say.

—What?

—You're concealing something from me.

—Of course; lots of things.

—No, I mean you are hiding something with industrious concealment.

—You are instructed to find it out?

—Yes; but, as you must know, the information is such that I needed no instructions to pursue it.

—How have you got on?

—Pretty far. I thought I would ask you; for your satisfaction as well as my own. It's that vehicle, or vehicles.

—I know.

—Well, what's your decision?

—They called the class: internal combustion machines.

—Vacuum produced by explosion of gas, said Dlar. What's the other principle?

—Revolving shaft. Now I should have to think.

—Don't trouble, let the engineers do their own work.

—It's better.

—I can see, Dlar mused, that it must have been an accursed thing.

Park was opening his mouth to say something; but so slowly that Dlar said:

—Do you prefer to go lower or up?

—Oh, up.

Oli came to Park.

—Remember, said Dlar, with a last anxious warning, that Oli is worth every forbearance.

Drak was a little tired of this.

—What is Oli? he asked, to conceal his impatience.

—Officially, head of the translations; socially, everywhere accepted; personally, a cultured man; intellectually, formidable. There he is; let's go in the vestibule.

Oli was gigantic with fur, clothing never worn by the black classes. He had a complete set of top clothes made of skin-lined skins, excepting only belt and collar. Many peninsular bears must have contributed to his astounding aspect; for feet, legs, hands and head were all swathed, as well as his body.

Whether it was Dlar's foresight or the servants' knowledge, as Oli was divested of his furs the giant woman-butler was at hand with a quilted cloak, possibly a more usual garment for ladies. Oli did not wince.

Nor at table or at ease did he show any recognition of peculiar attentions: queer drinks, some hot; oil served to him at table, as a sauce which he used with everything.

—I have tried maniacally, said he, to get hold of that report, the draft, or proof, or office copy; but whenever I caught it it was somewhere else. You cannot dry your hands with an eel. So here I am with wet and empty hands.

The three went into the library; blazing fire, well-arranged screens, all the little collection of books flat on the table, on which was a dish of hellebore. Oli took in all the dispositions. He showed first interest in the wonderful Summa Theologica; and without vanity gave a specimen of his knowledge.

Impossible to say whether his appreciation of the inside or the outside were more intricate; from codices and editions to the names and antecedents of the artists and binders whose work they beheld.

All this time, as the event proved, he was judging what should be his own contribution to the library Park was forming.

He found much to approve of; for Svillig, Koti, Edni the Prince, even little Toni, had been behind Park's desires and tastes; and old Dr Eza, his unmerciful friend, and many a learned man and scientific body had shown deserved gratitude for generous trouble Park had placed at their service; even taxing his poor musical gifts, and worse musical memory, when people grave enough desired him to do so.

At length Oli loitered at the manuscript book in which the owner was in process of writing out, at Reni's request, sentences of literary interest and poems which he was able to remember.

Oli thought aloud:

—As handwriting, cursive . . .

—Of my period, said Park, maliciously; remembering unnumbered conflicts.

—Of your period, said Oli, also remembering. You could show me (another time) the derivation from the uncial which preceded?

—There has been another uncial?

—Oh, yes.

—I could do what you ask; and, I think, display a number of stable intermediate forms.

—That would be most acceptable.

Caprice of memory had determined what the scrap-book should contain; Drak's inclination was to include every-thing he could remember which had any good quality. He blushed for its character of morceaux choisis. There was

> Captain or colonel or knight at arms,

facing

> Hear, my beloved, an old Milesian story.

—You may yourself have written one or the other of those poems, said Oli; but not both.

—The question is easier solved than that.

—I see.

As this was not at all Dlar's way of looking even at poetry, he burst a diversion.

—Turn over a bit, said he, to that sonnet; and he himself declaimed:

> When forty winters shall besiege thy brow,
> And dig deep trenches in thy beauty's field.

How he laughed.

—I believe that the poet means fifty-five when he writes forty; what do you think?

—That it is first-rate, said Park hotly.

—You mean desperately poetical.

Oli refused to be engaged, seeing as he thought a violent quarrel rapidly rising; and to all appeals weakly shrugged his narrow shoulders.

—I mean, said Drak, that it is sober and adequate as poetical expression.

Assertions & contradictions were certainly growing warm.

—If you people, said Park, know who the man is . . .

—Who the man is? How do you mean?

—Yes, is; I mean is.

Both remained silent a long time, while Oli struggled with the sonnet to get the sense.

There could be no question of deliberation when Park began very slowly:

—A military man . . .

He realized that, on three counts at least, he had said enough and too much. He looked at Reni and saw that he thought so too. The look was that mixture, possible only in unimprovable friendship, of defiance and confidence of indulgence; yet not without misgiving.

Dead Reni reflected. Then he said, in English:

—Park, you got me. I confess I did think the field was a ploughed field. Remember I am a farmer.

All laughed, while Park was struck with the abyss between black and white. But Oli, thrilled by the atmosphere of erudition, said also in English (and who could blame him for speaking sententiously):

—That poem was written at the beginning of sea-power.

The butler came and said, gigantically:

—The noblemen must hurry their bath to be in time for the prayer.

During supper Reni interjected, though it was a pity to leave all the trails that had been opened:

—Sea-power.

—Yes, said Oli; those toddling cargo-boats were sailing from port to port very much like ours, I have no doubt. Then the pirates met them, just as if they had run into a fog or an iceberg; and there was . . .

With that he looked at Park, who finished the sentence:

—dirty business.

—After that the pirates met other pirates.

Park and Reni laughed.

—Fleets, cargo fleets, fighting squadrons; better ships, heavier weapons; maps of the sea, wonderful navigation.

—Go on, said the dead men.

—Perfection at last, with the application of mechanical force, such as no one will ever know. Is it true?

—Yes, said Park.

—Wealth, pride, envy, until the sea was scored in every direction like a dark engraving. Do I exaggerate?

—No.

—As equality is only an idea, the sea-power belonged at length to one navy; and what became of it?

—What became of the others? you mean.

—Also, said Oli; and stopped.

—What did become of that sea-power?

—It is supposed, said Reni, that our occupation of territory was a matter of months, I mean rather than of centuries; for it took centuries to consolidate all. It was a struggle against those inexterminable men. I can only tell you what is plausible, and in harmony with the known conclusion.

—Which is what?

—We came to an unholy understanding with Belial; who got nothing out of it; for the two fleets at last went drifting and fighting into the unknown seas.

—No sea was unknown.

—Known or unknown, there they went; & there they remain.

—Believe me, the ships we are interested in are floating still, Park asserted recklessly.

—It is strange that you should say so, said Oli; for if ever merchant ships are swept into that region, added to the natural horrors men hear hideous explosions; and, close against them in the fog, grey towns pass, with their citadels over-towering.

—With lights? asked Park.

—No; no lights.

—And sound?

—Nothing but the sound of men singing.

They thought they heard clatter; and at the same time came the announcement:

—A mounted message.

It was startling, for the night was well through. A man entering busily, just as he had ridden, still in his cloak & helmet. The three men sprang to their feet at the sight of A Ra's badge. They all recognized the equerry.

—His Highness, said he, using less formality, commands Park to sup with the household on Nativity Eve, and to continue a member of it until His Highness's pleasure is fully known.

Park treated the messenger as though he were the sovereign, and said:

—At once.

Swiftly and easily, with few syllables it was understood that nothing but the usual rest, and a little refreshment, was required.

—We have with us unridden horses.

Park and Reni, in the movement of hospitality, snatched the time to compose the formal reply.

Oli gleaned a little gossip.

Reni became like a proud mother to his exotic friend, as he called him in his thoughts, though he never used the words nor any like them.

To put himself in Park's place as guest of the prince

taxed even his judgment and imagination. No such rough rule as 'Do nothing', 'Look pleased', 'Do what you are told to do', could satisfy him as friend, artist, magnanimous dead man.

He wished Park to arrive in the palace appropriately ignorant, and depart chastened. He wished all his demeanour, acts and words for three days to satisfy expectations & wear a finish of nicety. It was none of his wisdom to impose lessons in deportment and he considered it his part for a week to speak and act and think and be such that, supposing in Park the intelligence he had no temptation to doubt, he might pass through the ordeal in a manner worthy of himself and his tutor and yet think that he had been spontaneous all the time.

He began.

Leaving Oli asleep they went to mass on foot through the snow; and after getting a drink at a croft, they mounted the horses that met them; and spare horses followed unled, making for Reni. It was a still day.

The reader desiring to follow their route might take Bartholomew's map and find Minchinhampton. Park was between the villages of Cherrington and Rodmarton. They took the direction Crudwell, Minety, Swindon (as they saw it, a ravishing district, quietly undulating, cultivated without rapacity and beautifully wooded). Reni was to the eastern edge of it at the place now called Ashbury. Dlar had a fine enough view from his house, particularly from the roof, but the glory of the situation was the down, above to the south, where he and his friends could ride and gallop their fill.

—How I should like to cross the sea with you, Drak, he said as they rode.

Park looked at him and made no answer.

—We could get the permission. Short sea-crossing from the mouth of the Esi: then it is an incomparable ride east to the cornland. There are abundance of great, old-fashioned farms, all timber and brick; such hospitality; cultivation varied and delightful.

Park was staring.

—We should have to cross the cornland by train; not very agreeable. Then once over the mountains we are in the horse country.

—Is that agreeable?

—In a higher, bigger and better way, it is.

—What is there there?

—Nothing but horses. All our horses come from there.

—Are the men black?

—No, no, no; but very good fellows; so rough and simple; ways and language of their own.

—No black men?

—Only by chance; you will see. I mean, if we go.

—Haven't you to be born to a life like theirs? For what we mean by culture must be absent.

—Of course, but think of the compensations; the roughness, wildness & privation; sleeping on the ground in all weathers; and wild jobs in the dark.

—Respect for black men?

—Respect for horsemanship.

—It's not quite the same thing.

—No, & they think they are on an equality. They are a tough lot.

They rode into the Reni yard; bathed and changed; and went into the library to look at the treasures.

Dlar was engraving a plate, a whirlwind of animals in motion. He detected Park's faint smile as he showed him the design, and said:

—Coye'i.

—I like it, said Park.

—You do? And he considered it himself, absorbed.

Park began reciting:

> It is an ancient mariner,
> And he stoppeth one of three . . .

—Yes, said Reni; go on with your memories; and I'll be putting in a few scratches.

—If only I might remember it; it is long.

But as he tried, and jotted down fragments, he was thinking of this gentle existence in comparison with the wild life of the steppes.

For at Reni there was uncommon elegance.

WHERE Park set down was a long way from the palace; though the yard was above some of its depths. There was prodigious movement of carriages, horses, drivers and grooms. He was quickly picked out; led through the coping and across the grass to the entrance of a passage to that part of the palace where his business lay.

The servant who took him over walked before him until he met the officer appointed to entertain him. This gentleman had with him, beside his own attendants, Park's principal servant for his stay.

Park had to say whether he would rest; & elected to be guided by the steward.

—The five corridors off this gallery, said he, are ours, guests and stewards, inclusively and exclusively. We will, if you please, make a journey in other directions.

This consisted of visits to great and greater rooms of state, reached by corridors it was a pleasure to be in, for the sake of their austere design, & the opportunities they afforded to look down stairways which would have baffled Piranesi. The structure of the rooms was almost all that Park could attend to; but his inquisitive glances at particular objects did not escape his guide.

For in a circular apartment with a top light, the old steward slackened his steps as though it were a destination. It contained statues, human figures, just above life-size, single & groups of two, archaic in feeling, and each representing a restrained movement. All the faces were expressive; and the more so from being fitted with naturalistic eyes of different material; & teeth too, if there was occasion. The statues were of various material: hard stone, natural wood, perhaps metal; for one was enamelled all over. Some were painted in polychrome, but without naturalism.

Park looked at the works with leisure, as though the steward had ceased to exist; and this appeared to be right.

The next apartment visited contained works of art in the flat, like the sculpture subordinated to the general aspect of the room. The content was unspeakably over-rich. Park felt he would need to be appointed custodian of the gallery ever to comprehend what it contained. Moreover Toni Ra came in and greeted him familiarly.

Together they passed to a gallery of pottery. Park could not have contained his wonder; but the hum for prayer was heard, and all stood motionless.

Toni's white eyes fixed Park steadily under his coral eyebrows; so he made the sign of the cross and led the prayers. The steward knelt, but the prince remained standing. The steward from the folds of his garment produced a metal card and handed it to Park, who read from it the prayer for the archprince and his house.

Park was led back to his servants.

One more interpretation of an invariable programme, the evening passed never more rapidly. The last flush of the banquet had died from the youngest cheek. Someone in the character of M.C. made the announcement:

—Assembly in the Hall of Pillars, in silence & unattended; with four exceptions. His Highness, on appearing, will proceed at once, attended by the princes, to his place in choir. All present follow in the order of their precedence: they will be directed in the cathedral by the masters of ceremonies.

Park & another had particular directions to follow last.

In silence all moved to their quarters, for one purpose to

re-appear in freshly prepared clothes and new shoes.

Owing to his allotted place in the procession, Park found himself in the Hall of Pillars at the foot of the steps by which the prince would descend.

He was fat. His clothes were dazzlingly white. His shoes were tied round his bare ankles. He wore no badge, nor other ornament that Park could see. He passed evenly down the hall, followed by the princes, by the whole household.

The Hall of Pillars was very deep down; and yet it was a long descent; for the cathedral was entered at floor level. At the exit of the palace there was a tent erected, passing through streets, as Park supposed; for about a mile, as he judged. Feet made scarcely a whisper, and there was silence in the bowels of the earth.

When Park and his companion reached the cathedral door, they were taken by a sacristan to the chapel where they were to vest; for they were to be the acolytes.

Park, like a drowning man, abandoned himself to the space and the crowd.

There seemed to be plenty of time.

The procession formed. Park, with his restless, distracted habit, had begun by noticing the types, the linen, the vestments, the processional cross, the candlestick he himself carried; until, moved with contrition, he said to himself:

There is nothing more beautiful nor more terrible than the mass; and, with eyes downcast, he went about his business as an acolyte.

On the way to the altar the antiphon pealed: Ecce sacerdos magnus.

The bishop, he reflected; and that was all.

He recalled his days as a student in Rome, when he had assisted at great functions; and felt happy.

One feature affected him deeply, the genuflection at the words Et incarnatus est; but it always did.

But then another. When the credo had been sung, priests

91

in stoles came before the altar for reverence; there were hundreds of them; and dispersed by great groups in all directions of the church. He supposed that they were going to administer the Bread of Life to that world of famished souls. And with that he went to carry wine and water to the deacons.

After the ministers, the sovereign & the other princes, nobles and gentlemen knelt and received Holy Communion at the stretched cloth. When all had risen, Park observed that the deacons moved with the cloth down towards the entrance to the sanctuary. The acolytes took their torches to accompany the bishop and the assistant priest.

It was one child kneeling on the step, whose face was the colour of an altar-bread, with shut eyes, and streaming black hair, with lips and tongue like a rose.

—Corpus Domini nostri Jesu Christi custodiat animam tuam in vitam aeternam amen.

Park served private masses all night. At one of them his fellow-server was the archprince.

At some time or other a stranger found him and rescued him with the brief words Come on. He then first realized his fatigue, if not exhaustion. For four hours his poor, wrung heart had been filled with the love of Christ.

—I seem to want something, he said; a wash, I think.

—Food, air, said the stranger without ceremony.

Once outside the cathedral, they ran through the deserted covered way, and up those stately steps, three at a stride.

The stranger stayed with him until he was ready and then led him rapidly he knew not where. There was a din of talk in the great apartment.

—Just stand near His Highness, said the stranger.

Such is our common descent that in a minute all distinction of race and time, but not quite ever of rank, was gone. Talking rapidly, the prince, ignoring proffered trays, went to the sideboard to discover and extinguish appetites.

Catching Park's eye, he pointed with his fat, black finger to a morsel, which Park took and ate. He kept repeating this action; till Park had to laugh, and he laughed too.

—Come to the library, he said.

As he moved to the door, he called out:

—Where are all those men? Where's Edni? Where's Uncle Zi? Where's Koti? Where's the bishop? Where's Na'a? Toni, where are you? Where's Monsignor Villa? Where's the general? Where (with the faintest pause) is Reni?

They'll find 'em. Come on.

In the library he changed; enough for Park to recognize in him a student.

Books, judging by analogy, must have been there; but only on the table were any to be seen. The prince walked up to a pile, evidently from its neatness placed there by his orders.

—These should interest you.

—They do indeed, sir.

—Read the little one, he said, there's only one copy; this one is the big report, the others are appendixes.

Park did as he was told. A good many men came in. Someone brought him a lectern to support the book; for it was a folio. He read fast:

P. the subject is a normal human being. (He synopsized as his eyes tore over the pages.) His body is complete, except that he has lost four teeth, unfortunately not re-placed; slightly bald, good sight and hearing; intelligence fair; most of his reactions good.

He is presumed to be well educated according to some unknown system. He is believed to have knowledge of other languages beside that which he speaks by birth. He speaks base Latin; & this has proved most convenient for ready communication with him until he has learned Bapama: but true knowledge of that language he cannot be said to possess. His knowledge of religion is wide and orthodox.

Whatever other learning he possesses cannot, without injustice to the subject, be judged by comparison with Bapama standards: but he may be safely described as a cultured man, for he responds to tests which only a cultured man could satisfy.

He recognizes at once the good qualities of buildings & other works of art, even showing at times some little refinement. He can draw; but only indifferently well.

He is courageous, modest, perhaps diffident; he is bad tempered; he is truthful, with some power of dissimulation; but here allowance is due to his peculiar position. He has a sense of humour; and, among men he trusts (and his nature is affectionate), he is often vivacious.

He is not known to have any vices. However, in this connection traces have been discovered adhering to his teeth, of a substance which has not been identified; & the same is found in abundance in some dry vegetable remains which he had in his possession; and even more in an instrument through which it was used (or abused) by him.

The vegetable remains, putrid, were enclosed in a bag of very great interest.

Long descriptions of Park's clothing, noting the entire absence of linen.

Interesting chronometer with curious applications of mechanical principles already known, with one exception (unintelligible to Park, as described).

The subject's account of himself agrees in part with these observations.

So much Park gleaned, missing a great deal as though he had the hope of seeing the book again.

The question of his origin has been, & will be further studied. The appendixes treat of it. As to the place, his allegations are totally denied as untenable; they appear in his sworn statement (Appendix I). As to the time, his statements are (same Appendix) two in number; both absurd; insanely irreconcilable; and more so with the fact, whatever it may prove to be.

Hypotheses are almost as many as the persons who have advanced them.

That which is favoured by the best intelligence is (with permission) somewhat as follows:

The subject was born about 300 years ago, in some remote community, probably mountainous, for mountains have a peculiar and exhilarating effect on the subject, unknown to the infidels, for it is probably in their territory, where religion and culture have, Deo adiuvante, survived.

He may have been a theocrat; for it is the firm opinion of all who have interviewed him that he is, as he believes himself to be, a priest; and the possession of a chronometer by a man found almost in rags is significant.

The supposition is that through some great misadventure, whether vicious & excessive indulgence (favoured), bereavement, crime, disgrace, fear of torture, or rash psychic experiment (extremely favoured), he came under the domination of a remote ancestral survival in his consciousness; so thoroughly that he acts, speaks, thinks, and remembers in the person of that ancestor.

This hypothesis offers the best suggestion of how he reached Ia & why he came hither. He would have been impelled to return to the place of his origin as indicated by his hallucination.

Thorough enquiry has not found the least trace of evidence that his presence in the island was known to anyone until Edni Ra's servant arrested him. Though the suggestion is bewildering, it is that he arrived with fruit, which was unloaded in enormous bulk at this time, at one of the wharves of the Kottatil; got ashore in the darkness, and made his way under cover of plantations and hedges to the spot on the low down where he was detected. This is the least hazardous part of the conjecture, for he is a stealthy & powerful walker. He was not hungry when Cuan Niger found him; but, according to the man, very tired.

The rapid survey, under the peculiar conditions, and the objective view of his own character, stiffened Park's spirit, quieted his nerves, & strengthened his dignity. But the voice of the prince awoke him from deep abstraction.

—It's good, eh?

—Yes, sir; it is good.

—Filled with error, I suppose.

—Yes, sir; so far as I am competent to judge.

—You shall tell me about it. I have not yet visited Park. They tell me you have already a charming library. Some part of this report should be added to it. It cannot be what you have been reading; for that was prepared specially for me. The state paper (however excusably) is offensive. You shall have the appendixes, all of them, and none of them are accessible to the public; for, as pure scientific observation, they are worthy of a scholar's attention.

The library was filled with men. Something was forward, and Park alone seemed not to know what it was. At a signal the prince moved, and the whole crowd followed him up steps. Svillig came near Park and whispered:

—Dlar is here.

—Hulloa Svillig; is he? What is to happen?

—Dancing.

From the vestibule they came into the air, the Princes' Court. There was a carriage standing; and facing it an escort of scouts with lances. Behind the royal carriage were others in two ranks, round half the enormous circumference. The prince and a very old man got into the carriage. The scouts trotted ahead, all the other carriages moved. Very quickly all were rattling out into the blue of the frosty day. It was so fast and jolly that there was a certain amount of overtaking. The chilly tried to cover their heads and hide their hands. The road beggared Edni's in all respects; & much engineering had gone to its construction. Park was with Koti Ra.

—You have made an extraordinary impression on the

prince, he said. This expedition is supposed to be due to you, he added.

Park made no reply.

—Well, believe that you are going to enjoy yourself.

—Yes, said Park, recovering; I do and will.

—That's right. Reni is here.

—So I understand.

Koti talked so kindly.

—We are going to a college of young people, boys and girls. It is a very old college. Villa and Reni were both there. So was I, though you might not believe it; for the children are all beautiful. So was the prince.

—All beautiful?

—Yes, said Koti, gravely; a peculiar type sometimes appears among us, noticeable for one thing by the colour of the hair. They are called three-blood children.

—You interest me.

—I thought I should. The young people are never mated.

—Why?

—It is believed that such a union would be unfruitful.

—They marry others?

—Why, yes; I am married. Many receive sacred orders or enter religion. Some remain unmarried.

—That is not disapproved?

—No, you must respect the heart.

There was a spacious dancing platform with an inclined approach to it from the side of the college buildings; on the other a stand for spectators. The children were seen pouring out to the verandah, the girls chiefly distinguishable by their greater size.

A sort of glorified carpenter came and surveyed the scene; & had the awning drawn so as to have half and half light and shadow on the dancing floor. A crowd of children came tripping, bouncing, stamping upon it; & a big girl at once ordered most of them off.

The little orchestra came strolling, girls with flutes, a boy with a fiddle and another with cymbals.

The last gave a bang. Eight children performed a most slovenly reverence to the prince and lined up with a good deal of care and inaudible whispering.

Park supposed, correctly, that they did not wish to stare at himself, however briefly, under whatever pretext; for he was at the prince's left, with Reni on his other hand. And the prince gave him a knowing glance.

The dance was not Hunsdon House; but all the same it was the authentic deathless tradition, with which time had not played too many tricks; though there was a peculiarity most fatiguing for the dancers: whenever a boy had a stamp, he doubled it. Park was thrilled; and neither of his neighbours spoke.

The children knew they were doing well from the start; and they danced with more and better swing until they were up to the very edge of restraint, & all knew it was the last dance.

The prince beckoned, oh, so slightly; and, although no face was turned towards him, two boys ran over to him; then a few more; then all the children were round him, laughing and chattering. After a little they scattered among all the spectators.

As the prince walked across to the college followed by everybody, two porters were seen coming obliquely with a princely crate of oranges, and others with bulging baskets.

The prince made himself no more than an extra big boy.

—Let's have Dom Reni's song, said he; the Lark.

—Out of doors, the children shouted.

Out they went; and, standing on the frozen grass, they lifted their lovely faces to the zenith, & sang; the song dying away.

—Isn't he coming down? asked the prince, to break the emotion.

—Oh, do let him stay up, it's so blue, said a very little boy; and flung himself into the hands of the prince.

On the road back Edni, with whom he drove, spoke very guardedly to Park of the kind of life led by members of the household.

When he left, with Reni, to return to Park, he received an increase of rank.

THE WINTER was a happy time. The cultivation interested the owner of Park, and he gave as much time to his farm as did Reni to his. There was a succession of visitors, either at Reni or Park, to extend the intellectual activities of the two friends. Many celebrities remained no more than names. Dlar knew what he was abóut; by no means did mere position ever penetrate to either yard.

If celebrities came unbidden they were marvellously entertained, more mortuorum, as Reni said grimly.

A tomb is a very exclusive apartment.

It was different when A Ra's hinted visit occurred. For court reasons there was a bunch of them then. But the prince knew how to keep them in their position of furniture; and used his knowledge.

A waggon-load of entertainment accessories was the only announcement; and some packages addressed to Park. The books were varied; and each showed clearly enough who had made selection of them. Thus:

A sumptuous Vulgate; a complete breviary; the great dictionary; the history of dancing; a classic on farm management; portfolios of engravings; and the promised appendixes. It recalled to Park his first miserable little mail, when he lay wounded and terrified in what he knew now to have been a hovel.

Sentimentally, and in itself, the best thing that came over was a portrait of A Ra. It was a metal plate with metal inlay & enamel as to its substance. Drawing, massing, colour and quality were superb. The artist had treated the model with a freedom which, in Park's judgment, beyond others was the supreme merit of the work. And yet, among all men, actual and possible, it was the portrait of A, hereditary prince and vassal of his lordship the Emperor. The marvel was that a living man should be portrayed in a manner to which age and rarity would add no charm. What, mused Park, holding his breath with fear, might not the portrait of the Emperor be. But a black mind allowed itself no such imaginings. As he hoped to have a black mind, he dismiss-ed those imaginings piously and resolutely.

The picture exactly fitted the principal panel in the library; and he had it placed there, no longer wondering at miracles of prevision and contrivance. The afternoon sun did splendours upon the plate as the sovereign walked into the room & raised towards it his mild white eyes.

Park bowed his head in silence; & that was what was wanted.

PLEASANT academical evenings, as Reni ironically called them, took time. He would go with him, to share Park's suffering. Stupid cordiality, offensive praise, there was no fee the 'bodies' would not pay; but the 'extramurality' (Reni's term) of the proceedings enraged the lecturer. Passionate, servile appeals came even from distant cities, with hints of academical honours; but further than Ito he would not go; nor even there unless he had the big theatre of whatever 'body' it was; and no one addressed him unless addressed.

—If I don't know English, he would say in the tongue to Reni, I am not a dead man. The muck those fellows talk.

—You ought to be D.C.L., Reni would answer, to egg him to speak even more to the point.

But Kottatil!

Ah, Kottatil was a different place; a stuffy, different place, old Kottatil. Any boy there could draw Park's portrait on the wall; and many did. It was an art centre.

Thus those dead men amused themselves with bitter words.

PARK came to the chalk down. There were some new horses & the weather was open. Reni was nervously bright.

—You've heard about Svillig? No, of course you couldn't. You'd left home.

—What?

—He's a bishop.

—Bishop. What was he?

—At any rate not prince archbishop of Kano.

Park made as though to scream.

Reni said with a terribly nervous laugh:

—Not Kano the great, you unimaginable lunatic. I mean Kano of Istia.

Park didn't know what to answer.

—It has not gone at all well with that man Cuan.

Park showed his sadness at bad news added to Reni's insulting words.

—Where is he?

—In the islands.

No answer.

—It's not your case only, but lots of things. Come, Drak, we must be great, great, great friends. I was thinking a good thought. I was thinking that after the bath we will sing vespers. I will have every soul on the estate. We shall all like it, poor people. Largire lumen vespere.

—Right, Reni. It's the Forty Martyrs of Sebaste.

—I was not thinking of it: but that, as it happens, is the dedication of my oratory.

If capricious, this was the true Reni; for he was devout. How different from his then frame of mind, like that of a man expatriated!

—Park called, said the maid.

He went to the speaking room.

—Is it Drak?

—Yes, Monsignore.

—Svillig, Drak, if you please.

—We are very much upset.

—Be kind to Dlar; that's all.

He showed himself on the blue plate.

Far on in the night Reni said:

—That Cuan, you know; he has done nothing really wrong; it's only an accumulation. Edni thinks a great deal of him. He will be back before others.

As a flash of lightning reveals the unknown relation of visible things: the mountains close at hand, the river high above its supposed bed, Park's mental view became clear.

—Dlar, said he, if you go to the horse country, I go too.

—That's not a black thought, said Reni; beside, don't use your prophetic gift.

—So be it.

—That's more like it. We gallop in the morning.

—Let's gallop now.

—It's still too dark. The horses will be horribly afraid of us as it is.

After breakfast Reni said:

—I have to be a week in Kottatil.

—Do I go?

—No, I'll ride with you to Park.

PARK, in the absence of his friend, forgot the anger he shared with Reni, which perhaps was inspired by him; anger because he was not offered even a lectureship by the leakiest henroost of a university.

But his own he could not forget.

He rode, indignantly unattended, to the Charterhouse, and announced himself. The prior invited him into a cloister, in which they walked, in silence as the rule required. At the opening, he led into the garden and took

102

the first long path. Without preamble:

—Whatever impression I may have given you, I intended finality at our last interview, and intended you to understand. I care for none of your quibbles, and I am not the ecclesiastical authority. If you are not in rebellion, my words will do you no harm; and if you are, they may do you good. Men come to the Charterhouse in a spirit you have never possessed. You will not find here an escape from worldly difficulties merely because you are unable to solve them in a way you would have preferred. A boy who has climbed to the top of the Ondo mast must not, because he cannot make up his mind to climb down, expect to find a trap-door in the sky. I do not like to risk offence by telling you what you know; but for men of every position & every origin there is only one way to peace: purification of the heart, and the proper direction of the energies. You understand me.

—I want peace, Father.

—Persevere in that wish, my son.

—At least, give me your blessing, Father.

—God bless you.

Fine order the Carthusian, Park reflected.

The prior gave him a precious book: Pharetra divini amoris.

He rode to the Carmel near his home. He had been twice in a parlour, but had never spoken to the prioress.

—Deo gratias, said the voice.

—Deo gratias. I am speaking to the mother prioress?

—Yes.

In the silence which followed he felt sure the nun was praying. He thought first of naming himself; and then that it was unnecessary. Instead he said:

—I have need of prayers; many and great prayers.

—We have only one instrument, and it is prayer.

—Do you pray for the dead?

—Yes, very much. For the living also.

—Will you pray for Park of Park?

—I do. I began to do so on the feast of the Assumption.

—Will you continue?

—Yes. I am sure you will pray for us. We need prayers.

HE WENT to mass long before dawn. Immediately after he mounted and rode to Edni's villa. By this time it was light. Edni was from home, and there were no guests. He had some breakfast and formed the sudden resolution to take a walk, a remedy he had never tried.

He borrowed a pair of farm boots and set out in a northerly direction. It was the most lovely of spring days; & he walked on slowly, recovering his soul. What a world! The hedges were still white with fruit-trees in flower and the ground was wild with celandine, wood anemone, violets, some primroses. He came about eighteen miles; for he always thought in that measure and decimally; and was overlooking one of the courses of the young Thames, as he secretly called it: the Windrush and Swinbrook. It affected him as the natural scene did under that sort of restorative fatigue.

He moved along the top edge of the valley, gently rocked in his spirit by the circumstances: the light, the loneliness; when it struck him that something was going a bit too far. He thought he would sit down, or perhaps lie down. He had sometimes foolish apprehension about his heart.

He heard a long musical note, which made him think he was ill. He had the illusion of false memory, and seemed to be predicting the sounds which duly reached him. He felt someone was handling him. He or another said:

—I am afraid he is dead.

Another voice said:

—No, ma'am, he's not dead; I think he's been knocked down.

—Quick, Jenny: where's my bag?

104

Something was poured in his mouth.

—Do you feel better, sir?

—Melius habeo, he replied. He opened terrified eyes to see two ladies, one kneeling; and shut them again.

He was strongly raised to his feet and made to walk.

—It's no good, said the man; who lifted him by main force and set him down.

—Vernon, where's the nearest hospital?

—Ciren.

—Cizzeter, she corrected, having a mania of her own.

—Step out; but for heaven sake, take care.

The rhythm as they rolled along did Park good, & the musical note seemed pleasant. He smiled as he saw the kind faces of the ladies, sitting uncomfortably; & wanted to make a change.

—No, stay where you are. Which way were you going?

—I don't know.

Arrived at the town she spoke through the tube:

—Drive right on.

—I am taking you to a hospital; they are very nice.

—Thank you. And he gave up again.

More lugging and carrying and another seat. Someone felt his pulse. He tried violently to be himself.

—I am sure you will be all right.

—A thousand thanks. There was a prick in his arm.

—Keep still. You're all right. And he was alone.

—What's your name, sir?

—Dr Park.

—What's your address? He named his college.

—Well, I'll tell you what it is. You've no pain?

—None.

—I could telephone for the doctor: but I am sure there is nothing wrong with you. It's a very warm day, and you have taken a faint. If you like I could telephone to Mrs Jones for a room.

—Pardon me, Sister, what place is this?

105

—Malmesbury.

—Is it really? But I am staying with Mrs Poole.

—Then you're all right. Of course, it's Dr Park. How long have you been down?

—About a fortnight.

—Isn't it nice weather?

—I am as right as rain. Well, good-bye; so sorry.

—HULLOA, Dr Park, we thought you were coming back by the Fairford bus. Had you a nice walk? It's not too late for tea: it's only a quarter past five. Irene !

16th August, 1929

Dear Dr Park,

I do not think there is anything significant in what you tell me. Walk a lot: but I should not exceed twenty-five miles at one time if I could help it.

If, when you come in, you feel fatigue or are wet, take as usual five grains of each. If you felt inclined you could go back to your tablets for a few days.

I hope you have a good holiday.

Yours ever,

M.B., B.Sc.

LATER, the writer of this letter heard a reasoned abbreviation of the foregoing narrative, and commented it from his special point of view.

—You were asleep, said he; it was not a faint. It was a

short, deep sleep; and what you experienced was a waking state.

—A short sleep, said Park.

—But sleep is sleep, long or short.

—And a long dream.

—Somewhat more elaborate than is usual.

Afterword

I

SOME TIME in the early nineties John Gray wrote a short story, 'The Person in Question', which was found unpublished among his papers many years after his death. The story is a variation on a nineties theme — the *doppelgänger*. The narrator comes face to face with himself twenty-five years on, and is filled with fascination and repulsion for his double and the sort of female company he keeps. The narrator tries to naturalize the experience in terms of hallucination and mania, but it is his fascination with sin and his sense of guilt which make most impression on the reader.

The story can be seen as a coda to *The Picture of Dorian Gray* (1891) by his friend, Oscar Wilde. Indeed, there were rumours at the time that John Gray was the original Dorian of that name. He is certainly referred to as 'Dorian' Gray in the diaries and letters of William Rothenstein, Ernest Dowson and Lionel Johnson, and on one occasion signed himself 'Yours ever, Dorian' in a letter to Wilde. But when *The Star*, in a report of February 1892, made the same identification, it was obliged to issue an apology: even then it did not do to be so nearly associated with Wilde.

Whether John Gray was the original Dorian or not is still vigorously debated. Wilde and Gray are known to have been fellow guests at a dinner party early in 1889, but this is no evidence for friendship, which does not seem to have developed until after the first version of *The Picture of Dorian Gray* appeared in *Lippincott's Monthly Magazine* (July 1890). The aesthetes of the nineties would, no doubt, be amused at our attempts to link the real and the fictitious Gray; they would simply have enjoyed this example of nature imitating art, for John Gray was an uncommonly good-looking young man.

Again, we can only speculate on the nature of Gray's

relationship with Wilde. Amid the self-pity of Wilde's letter, *De Profundis*, from prison to Lord Alfred Douglas, there is the suggestion that it was platonic: 'When I compare my friendship with you to my friendship with such still younger men as John Gray and Pierre Louÿs I feel ashamed. My real life, my higher life was with them and such as they.'

Gray was born on 2 March 1866 in the working-class suburb of Bethnal Green, London. His father was a wheel-wright and carpenter, and Gray himself became a metal-turner at Woolwich Arsenal. He was interested in languages and studied Latin, French and German in his spare time. He was promoted to the drawing-office, but in 1882 he sat and passed the Civil Service entrance examination for a Lower Division clerkship. He worked in various departments of the Post Office until 1888 when he was transferred to the Foreign Office as a librarian, a job he kept until he left for Rome in 1898 to study for the priesthood.

He soon found his way into the literary and artistic circles of the nineties. In 1892 he was living in the Temple, in Plowden Buildings, on the same floor as the poet Arthur Symons and the translator Alexander Teixeira de Mattos; W. B. Yeats and George Moore were in the same building. Although never a member of the Rhymers' Club, Gray frequented their meetings and read his poems.

Another circle he moved in was that of the artists Charles Ricketts and Charles Shannon who founded the Vale Press. His first essays and stories appeared in their magazine *The Dial*, and one of the last pieces he wrote before setting off for Rome in 1898 was a prospectus for the Vale Press edition of Jules Laforgue's *Les Moralités Légendaires*, with engravings by Lucien and Esther Pissarro. It was Gray who had introduced Lucien Pissarro to Charles Ricketts.

Ricketts designed Gray's first book of poems, *Silverpoints* (1893), regarded by many as the quintessential nineties volume, the craftsmanship divided equally between the verse and the book design. The poems were set amid a wide expanse of margin; it was all very precious. Ada Leverson quipped with Wilde that he should go one step further and 'publish a book *all* margin; full of beautiful unwritten thoughts'.

His second volume, *Spiritual Poems*, came out in 1896 and, no doubt, reflected the crisis in Gray's personal life brought to a head by the arrest of Wilde the year before. Many of the poems are translations. The reader is struck by the frequent references to the various saints called John; we cannot help but read them as autobiography and an attempt to settle his spiritual identity. Again, a sense of guilt and expressions of remorse predominate.

Like Dowson, Gray had been much affected by the simple Catholicism he had observed among the French peasantry. After a visit to Brittany he was received into the Catholic Church in 1890, but seems to have lapsed almost immediately. Perhaps it needed the crisis of Wilde's arrest to force the issue of his religious life to a resolution.

In November 1892 Gray had met André Raffalovich. His parents were *émigré* Russian Jews who had settled in Paris. Raffalovich was wealthy and had moved to London ten years earlier. He was a year or two older than Gray and a patron of the arts. He was much exercised by the moral implications of his homosexuality and wrote numerous articles and pamphlets, as well as a substantial volume, on the subject. They remained friends for life. Whatever may have been the nature of their relationship at first, there is no evidence to suggest that it took a sexual form from the mid-nineties onward. In 1896 Raffalovich became a Catholic and two years later Gray made his decision to enter the priesthood: two formal acts which suggest bulwarks against the flesh.

Early in 1898 Aubrey Beardsley had died. Gray had met him through Raffalovich and the three became close friends. Gray and Raffalovich were instrumental in Beardsley's conversion to Catholicism, something for which they have suffered at the hands of the artist's biographers. In the last year of his life Beardsley was supported financially by Raffalovich. In 1904 Gray, now a curate in Edinburgh, edited *The Last Letters of Aubrey Beardsley*, a collection of the letters that Raffalovich and he had received from their friend.

Another friend made through Raffalovich was the Jesuit, George Tyrrell. He eventually fell foul of the ecclesiastical authorities and was excommunicated for his part in the Modernist movement in 1907. Raffalovich corresponded with Tyrrell for about ten years, and stood by him after his excommunication.

Raffalovich followed his friend to Edinburgh, and in 1907 Gray became rector of St Peter's, Morningside, the building of which was largely at Raffalovich's expense. The architect of this fine church was Sir Robert Lorimer; a painting of St Peter was done by Sir Frank Brangwyn, a friend of Gray's from the Fitzroy days of the Rhymers' Club.

From Edinburgh Gray renewed contact with Katherine Bradley and Edith Cooper, an aunt and her niece who lived together and wrote under the name 'Michael Field'. They, like Gray, seemed to feel the need to repent of all they had done and stood for in the years 1885-95. They, too, became Catholics.

Another Catholic convert Gray knew well was Eric Gill, the engraver, sculptor and type-designer. They corresponded and visited each other frequently over the years; in 1930 Gray officiated at the marriage of Gill's daughter Joanna and René Hague. The priest and the younger artist had much in common: a love of craftsmanship in engraving, printing, book design, stone-carving and sculpture. Gill and Hague, in fact, printed and designed the first edition of *Park*. The frontispiece was from an etching by

Denis Tegetmeier, Gill's other son-in-law. Through Gill, Gray met and became acquainted with the work of the artist and writer David Jones. Gradually, and never of course thoroughly, Gray was won over from the world of Ricketts and Shannon to that of Eric Gill and David Jones, although he kept in touch with Ricketts until the latter's death in 1931. Perhaps his appreciation of Beardsley had prepared the way for his appreciation of that other artist in black and white, Eric Gill.

After years of silence, Gray began publishing poetry again in the early twenties. His later verse shows that he has learnt some of the lessons of modernism; it is much more spare than his work in the nineties, but its idiom is more often Georgian than modernist.

Gray was a great walker, visiting the Cotswolds each summer for his holiday. Iceland was another favourite holiday resort. He wrote about these and other subjects in a series of essays, full of discriminating observations, which appeared in *Blackfriars,* a journal published by the Oxford Dominicans. The same journal began to serialize *Park* in late 1931 and early 1932, before it was published in book form in April of the latter year.

Over the years, Raffalovich entertained in his Edinburgh house many resident and visiting artists, writers and scholars: Henry James, Max Beerbohm, Gordon Bottomley, Walter Sickert, Compton Mackenzie, Herbert Grierson, Herbert Read. Gray would have known them all. He corresponded with Edmund Blunden and A. J. A. Symons, and met Eric Gill's friend, Desmond Flower, when the latter was on his quest for Dowson.

And then, in February 1934 Raffalovich died. Within a few months — on 14 June — Gray, too, was dead.

II

As a poet, Gray will probably be best remembered as a translator: he was essentially a craftsman whose imagination needed the impetus and discipline of a sound model. Through Wilde, Gray met Pierre Louÿs in 1892 and their friendship is recorded in a correspondence which has come down to us. In Paris Louÿs introduced Gray to Verlaine and Mallarmé and other Symbolist poets. In his translations of these writers, Gray was one of those nineties writers who was sowing the seed for the poetic experimentation of the next two decades. There is a poetic maturity in his translations which his own work often lacks, and which is evident in his version of Rimbaud's 'Charleville':

> The square, with gravel paths and shabby lawns.
> Correct, the trees and flowers repress their yawns.
> The tradesman brings his favourite conceit,
> To air it, while he stifles with the heat.
>
> In the kiosk, the military band.
> The shakos nod the time of the quadrilles.
> The flaunting dandy strolls about the stand.
> The notary, half unconscious of his seals.
>
> On the green seats, small groups of grocer men,
> Absorbed, their sticks scooping a little hole
> Upon the path, talk market prices; then
> Take up a cue: I think, upon the whole . . .
>
> The loutish roughs are larking on the grass.
> The sentimental trooper, with a rose
> Between his teeth, seeing a baby, grows
> More tender, with an eye upon the nurse.
>
> Unbuttoned, like a student, I follow
> A couple of girls along the chestnut row.
> They know I am following, for they turn and laugh,
> Half impudent, half shy, inviting chaff.

I do not say a word. I only stare
At their round, fluffy necks. I follow where
The shoulders drop; I struggle to define
The subtle torso's hesitating line.

Only my rustling tread, deliberate, slow;
The rippled silence from the still leaves drips.
They think I am an idiot, they speak low;
— I feel faint kisses creeping on my lips.

There is often something 'asiatic' (in Arnoldian phrase) about Gray's original compositions. The eroticism of 'The Barber', for all its heterosexuality, is utterly perverse, and its movement and rhythm mark it unmistakably as Decadent. It is the verbal equivalent of a painting by Gustave Moreau:

I dreamed I was a barber; and there went
Beneath my hand, oh! manes extravagant.
Beneath my trembling fingers, many a mask
Of many a pleasing girl. It was my task
To gild their hair, carefully, strand by strand;
To paint their eyebrows with a timid hand;
To draw a bodkin, from a vase of kohl,
Through the closed lashes; pencils from a bowl
Of sepia to paint them underneath;
To blow upon their eyes with a soft breath.
They lay them back and watched the leaping bands.

The dream grew vague. I moulded with my hands
The mobile breasts, the valley; and the waist
I touched; and pigments reverently placed
Upon their thighs in sapient spots and stains,
Beryls and crysolites and diaphenes,
And gems whose hard harsh names are never said.
I was a masseur; and my fingers bled
With wonder as I touched their awful limbs.

116

Suddenly, in the marble trough, there seems
O, last of my pale mistresses, Sweetness!
A twylipped scarlet pansie. My caress
Tinges thy steelgray eyes to violet.
Adown thy body skips the pit-a-pat
Of treatment once heard in a hospital
For plagues that fascinate, but half appal.

So, at the sound, the blood of me stood cold.
Thy chaste hair ripened into sullen gold.
The throat, the shoulders, swelled and were uncouth.
The breasts rose up and offered each a mouth.
And on the belly pallid blushes crept,
That maddened me, until I laughed and wept.

Both these poems appeared in *Silverpoints*. During the
years of his poetic silence, he had kept abreast of contemporary literature and learnt much that was to affect his own
technique. It is interesting to note, in the opening of *The
Long Road* (1926), the occasional phrasing and cadence
which we have come to associate with the later Eliot,
deriving in both cases, of course, from the liturgy:

In Thy Name and dread,
VIATOR, those who start at peace
with other men essay the ease
of measured stride and supple knees;
their road lies ahead.

The son of Israel
passed dryfoot through the cloven sea;
again, the wise mysterious three
were guided by the star to Thee.
May we journey well.

If thus things may be,
grant us, dispensed from all alarm,

```
        protected from conspicuous harm,
        to stretch at evening, fed and warm,
            and drink merrily;

            worn, resolute,
        to enter once, nor over late,
        in easy trim and blest estate,
        by that desired, eternal gate,
        where proffered cup and towel wait,
            and winged guards salute.
```

But that 'merrily' throws us back to the Georgians.

John Gray, then, is no W. B. Yeats, emerging from the world of the Rhymers' Club to become a major modern voice. But then, neither is he a Victor Plarr, Pound's Monsieur Verog in *Hugh Selwyn Mauberley*, living 'out of step with the decade' amid his pickled foetuses and *fin de siècle* memories.

III

Eric Gill commented to a correspondent: 'Yes, I have read "Park" and found it extremely interesting, it is a thoroughly weird business, typical of its author. I think there are very good things in it, and things that only a Catholic could have guessed at.' One would not wish to disagree.

Those critics who have written on *Park* have been reluctant to engage with the work further, contenting themselves with pointing to sources and models. Certainly, H. G. Wells's *The Time Machine*, with its division of a future England into two races, the surface Eloi and the subterranean Morlochs, is behind the topography of *Park*. In William Morris's *News from Nowhere* the protagonist is transposed in time, through a dream experience, from the Hammersmith of the nineteenth century to a Hammersmith in an idealized future. Richard Jefferies's *After London* tells of a pastoral England after some great cataclysm. E. M. Forster's story, 'The Machine Stops', provides a source for the speaking room. All these, and more, went into the making of Gray's fantasy. He drew from a wide range of literary, cultural and liturgical material: from Langland's *Vision of Piers Plowman* — where Langland has his dream vision of another, Pré-Reformation, theocratic England in the Malvern hills — to Fritz Lang's *Metropolis* (1927) and the religiosity of its vast, candle-lit cavern with Maria preaching to the subterranean work force.

Part of the weirdness the reader experiences is that he does not know whether to read the work as essentially utopian, dystopian or satirical. Here there is none of the straightforward satire of totalitarianism we find in Kingsley Amis's *The Alteration*, where English history is rewritten without the Reformation.

The correspondence of Edmund Blunden and John Gray sheds some light on this problem, as well as explaining a few incidental allusions. Blunden wrote in February 1933:

> . . . But your fantasy has astonished me, with that quality which the term hints but [which] seldom occurs in association with it. The very choice of 'Mungo Park', at this time of day, started me off in your strange world with intimacy; and then you gave a succession of inventions and illusions which held the convincing wild familiarity of dream experience. I am glad Drak's book had S. T. C.'s 'Hear, my beloved, an old Milesian story' — that poem especially. The world's most fascinating anagram has defeated me so far although I seemed on my way to the solution. The Latin, as far as the Melius habeo on p.126 has a strange effect; so one dreams fluently in an unaccustomed tongue, but with only short phrases in fact going on.

Gray replied later that month:

> . . . Your astuteness has penetrated the whole matter: the

man stumbling in his dream upon a chance of vengeance & the free expression of repressed ambitions, yet dogged all the time by the obstacles of his waking life.

The anagram is read from the sentence Ave Maria gratia plena Dominus tecum. It is made, as you see, to tease the mind of a man like Drak.

A mixture of satire and wish-fulfilment, then, with Park's feeling that he is dead and the mysterious commission of enquiry suggesting, perhaps, the obstacles of waking life.

But why is England (or the province of Ia) a theocratic state ruled by black men, with the indigenous white population living a rodent existence underground? Is this the aesthete Gray taking vengeance on industrial Britain? Certainly, we know from his sister that Gray was 'deeply interested in the black man (he was a keen anthropologist) and used to say, although he was a white man he was black inside; and he foretold in a general way that the black man would rule'.

Just as Thomas More had used Amerigo Vespucci's *Four Voyages* as a point of departure for writing *Utopia*, so Gray made use of Mungo Park's *Travels into the Interior of Africa* (1799). But to understand why Gray draws on Park's *Travels* we have to see it in conjunction with Melville's *Typee*, alluded to incorrectly in the text as *Three Years [sc. Four Months] in the Marquesas Islands*, the title of the first English edition of 1846. There, amid the narrator's account of his gradual realization that he was a prisoner in the valley of the Typees, appears a number of Rousseauist condemnations of missionary endeavour in the South Seas. Gray, in an early story, had satirized the missionaries, too. But his South Sea islander is shown to be far more cultivated than the missionaries. And the historical Mungo Park had found Africa quite other than the savage continent of popular imagination; he had even encountered Mohammedan negroes in West Africa practising as professional advocates in the tribal palavers, who were in no way inferior to counsel in the law courts of Great Britain. Gray's book is, in some respects, an answer to Melville's. He might agree with Melville about missionary abuses, but he did not share the American's illusions about the 'noble savage'. If the African could embrace Islam and make it his own, then Gray could imagine a black Christian civilization strong enough to supplant a degenerate white industrialism.

Gray's 'repressed ambitions' are everywhere in evidence. This is an ordered, hierarchic, and hieratic, world. Under the emperor, power among the Wapami is vested in A Ra, the archprince who is in sacred orders, his nephew Toni Ra, and the other hereditary princes and princess, Edni Ra, Koti Ra and I. It is a landed aristocracy to which Park, who explains his name as 'enclosed property', is admitted. There is no money in Ia; when Park buys a book it is charged against his crop. Of the spiritual hierarchy, Park has easy access to priors and prioresses, but not, interestingly, to the archbishop of Kottatil, a white man, glimpsed at a distance on his second day in Ia. Another who is conspicuous by his absence is the pope, never once referred to in this Catholic world.

Outdoors Park enjoys the Cotswold countryside, and indoors he shares another of Gray's pleasures, his love of finely-printed books and engravings. Much time is spent in the library, and this is one of the first rooms that guests are shown in Ia.

The bath is as much a regular feature of daily life as prayer. The outright sensuality of 'The Barber' has given way, in the description of Park's bath and massage at the hands of Cuan, to a simple sensuousness. *Typee* again provides a source. The native Kory-Kory carries the lame narrator to the stream, morning and evening, to bath him, and the girls of the house anoint him with oil. There is pleasure, too, in the new, loose-fitting toga which Park now wears, something which Eric Gill, with his polemics against trousers, would have endorsed.

A disturbing element, however, is the relative insignificance of women among the Wapami; a prioress, a silly princess and her even sillier attendants, the girls at the college, are the only female presences in this otherwise male enclave. This is to be attributed to Gray's homosexual temperament and the long habit of clerical celibacy, although it is evident that celibacy is not the universal rule among the clergy of Ia; the Vicar General is the great-grandfather of Svillig's great-grandfather. The college for the three-blood children is probably an allusion to the pre-Freudian notion of homosexuality as 'the third sex' and Raffalovich's advocacy of an early training for homosexuals in their responsibilities as 'superior uranians' who were to sublimate their sexuality in service to science, the arts or the Church.

The Wapami use familiar names and Park is known as Drak among friends. On formal occasions he is referred to as Kentigern, the Latin form of Mungo. Only Dlar is able to pronounce his surname with ease. He is an excellent scholar of English and takes interest in the passages of English verse that Park can recollect. A lay-brother has a few phrases, but otherwise, at least on the surface, English is dead. Not so, of course, Latin, the language of the Church, and Park is able to communicate with his captors quite easily in that tongue. The language of the Wapami is Bapama, with its singular, dual and plural forms, and gradually Park makes some progress in it. But Wapami numeration and chronology are a constant source of bewilderment and distress. In his *Travels*, Mungo Park records of the Bambarra: 'It is curious that in counting the cowries, they call eighty a hundred; whilst in all other things they calculate by the common hundred. Sixty is called a Manding hundred.' Gray has taken this Bambarra numeration over, and introduced it into Wapami chronology, too. The only sense of time that Park shares with the Wapami is liturgical time, the sequence of feasts of the

Church: the Assumption (15 August), All Souls' Day (2 November), the feast of St Gertrude, the thirteenth-century German mystic whose prayers Gray translated (15 November), Christmas, and the Forty Martyrs of Sebaste, Roman soldiers frozen to death in a fourth-century persecution in Turkey (10 March). He can explain the date 1777 only by reference to St Alphonsus Liguori, the Italian theologian and Doctor of the Church who was living at that time.

Park hears mass on the feast of the Assumption in a church dedicated to the Martyrs of Uganda, twenty-two African youths put to death between 1885-87 by the king of Buganda for refusing to submit to his homosexual demands. As he reviewed his own life in London during the same years, Gray would have been struck by the contrast.

The commission of enquiry, with its innumerable sessions, formal and informal, public and private, and the humorous displacements of its report on Park, is, no doubt, an expression of Gray's own sense of 'the obstacles of his waking life', many created by ecclesiastical authority. But it seems to point to a deeper anxiety, too. Everyone who meets Park feels certain that he is a priest, but this cannot be proved: he has no celebret, the commendatory letter necessary for a priest to be permitted to say mass in a church other than his own. Consequently, he is unable to function as a priest during his time in Ia, which is a cause of much distress to him. Perhaps not a crisis of identity on Gray's part, but certainly misgivings.

One of the most attractive features of *Park* is its irony and the many flashes of wry humour. The spareness of the writing and the rapid transitions generate much of this. The dream sequence of Westminster Cathedral as a railway station, with Park looking for the sacristy and a third-class smoking compartment, his server and a porter, is a sheer delight. Bentley's cathedral seems to provoke this sort of treatment; in Corvo's *Hadrian VII* (1904) it had been described as a 'pea-soup-and-streaky-bacon-coloured caricature of an electric-light station'.

The humorous account of the Dominican prior asking whether Park knew any Thomases among the Dominicans of his day, in an attempt to establish whether he had been a contemporary of St Thomas Aquinas, the great thirteenth-century theologian, is touched with a deeply-felt sense of tradition which gives the novel its most poignant moment. This is followed, almost immediately, by some deliciously sly humour. Park notices that the Dominican habit has remained unchanged, except for the bare feet. Clearly, the Dominicans have been in need of reform and, like those of the Carmelites who followed St Teresa and St John of the Cross, are now a discalced order.

The ecclesiastical world of the Wapami is decidedly pre-Reformation. All the great orders are there: the Benedictines (Svillig), the Cistercians (the tutor), the Carthusians (the prior), the Dominicans (the prior) and the Carmelites (the prioress). But where are the Franciscans? And is the Catholic Church conceivable without the Jesuits, the great order of the Counter-Reformation? Where are they? Have they been suppressed — again? Gray could hardly have overlooked the Franciscans and the Jesuits: they were his ecclesiastical neighbours in Edinburgh for many years.

The modern reader will, rightly, be curious about Gray's stance toward political and social questions. It has to be said that these are invariably left vague and unresolved. There is in *Park* none of More's openness in *Utopia* about the reluctant use of military force as a last resort. When Park asks whether the subterranean population is involved in military exercises the question is ignored. Later, Dlar admits that there is a military establishment for the empire, and that Ia is misleading in that its people are extraordinarily docile to good government. The enemy is the empire of Belial, the anti-Christ, which appears to be located around the Pacific Ocean, although whether it includes the

Philippines, with which the Wapami have trading connections, is not made clear. Again, Park's discussion with Dlar and Oli about sea-power is equally inconclusive. When Park asks whether the subterranean population is content, Dlar and Ini'in answer, with unconvincing promptness, in the affirmative. All this is, of course, registered through Park's consciousness; this is a novel, not a treatise on society. Park is often disturbed by what he sees and hears in Ia. When Cuan is prosecuted for shooting him, Park 'gulped down his misery'; when Svillig, the Vicar General's secretary, ordered the gladiatorial porters to clear a path for them with whips, he 'grieved'; and when he learns that Cuan has been sent to the islands, he resolves to accompany Dlar to the horse country. Clearly, something is wrong in this self-sufficient province of Ia, with its representative government and its observance of natural, positive and ecclesiastical law. The Marxist, no doubt, would give it short shrift; but then, Canon Gray would probably give the Marxist no shrift at all.

Although he knew well the radical Dominican, Vincent McNabb, Gray never seems to have been drawn to Distributism, the social theories of Chesterton and Belloc. Gray's focus was on the dire effects of industrialism rather than on the political and economic causes of the problem. There is, of course, a strong tendency to fatalism in such an approach, but utopian solutions are usually no more than pelagianism under a collective guise. The 'intolerable paradox' presented by the subterranean population — 'mechanical construction & genius we cannot overpraise, with moral degeneration the most complete' — may be bad social theory, but is probably sound social wisdom. Original sin was the bedrock of Gray's thinking on these matters. The spiritual needs of the conquered white population are ministered to solicitously; the surface cupolas look down on to sanctuaries far below ground. The archbishop, the learned Oli, head of translations, and the hideous Hil'nu, designer of the exquisite illustrations to the *Summa Theologica* with which Dlar presents Park, all emerge from their ranks: 'God is no respecter of persons'.

Catholicism does not so much provide a social doctrine, rather it is a social doctrine for Gray. Modern taste reacts against the fetishistic, nineteenth-century form his Catholicism took — Benediction, Exposition and Perpetual Adoration: the stock-in-trade of the nineties convert — but we cannot miss the note of simple faith in the description of Park's assistance at midnight mass. 'He supposed that they were going to administer the Bread of Life to that world of famished souls.' Here is none of that affectation which, in Wilde's novel, surrounds Dorian Gray's flirtation with Catholicism and his pleasure at watching the priest lift up the monstrance 'with that pallid wafer that at times, one would fain think, is indeed the "*panis coelestis*", the bread of angels'.

Park, then, and through him Gray himself, is sure in his faith, but can still feel the restrictions that that faith, especially in its institutional form, lays on him. Dorian is tamed, not dead. One of the prohibitions imposed on Park by the Tenure of Property, which comes with his estate, is against 'any exhibition of horsemanship'. Yet it is to the horse country, where the skills of horsemanship rather than black men are respected, that Park wishes to go when he hears of Cuan's temporary banishment to the islands. When Dlar had suggested a visit earlier, Park protested the absence of culture there. Dlar had urged the compensations of 'the roughness, wildness & privation', and desire for the wild life of the steppes seems to have overcome Park's reservations. Whether the yearning for freedom is purely personal or more general, encompassing the subterranean population as well as the black gamekeeper Cuan, is not made explicit. What is clear, however, is that Ia is no *cité harmonieuse*; but then it is no abiding city, either. And just as Roman Cirencester gave way, in time, to industrial Britain, and that in its turn was conquered by the Wapami, so Ia, too, will perish. The new Jerusalem is outside even liturgical time.

It is easy in discussing the themes of *Park* to lose sense of the strangeness of effect of Gray's prose. This does so much to sustain the fantastic in the novel, and is achieved, in part, by a precision in diction and a terseness of expression. This becomes, perhaps too readily, a mannerism, the aesthete fastidiously seeking *le mot juste*. At its most successful, however, Gray's prose has a decidedly modernist ring to it. The impression, at times, is of a literary costiveness. And while critics of a psychoanalytical bent will, no doubt, have elucidations of their own to offer for this, Dr Peter Vernon's suggestion that Gray's early training in the Civil Service may have left its mark on his style has much to recommend it.

Paradoxically, the modernism of Gray's prose is most apparent when he is relying on scholastic modes of thought. The intellectualism of the Post-Impressionist world was prefigured, in some respects, by the intellectualism of St Thomas; something, of course, which did not escape the notice of the master modernist, James Joyce.

A thoroughly weird business, then, shot through with a Catholic imagination, *Park* certainly has very good things in it.

A note on the text, and further reading

Park was first published in 1932, in a limited edition of 250
copies. A second edition, limited to 350 copies, with an
introduction by Bernard Bergonzi, was published in 1966.
Paragraphing and quotation marks were omitted in both
these editions. Paragraphing and the use of the dash to
indicate dialogue have been introduced in this edition.

Books

Cevasco, G.A., *John Gray*, Boston, 1982

Sewell, Brocard (ed), *Two Friends*, Aylesford, 1963

Sewell, Brocard, *Footnote to the Nineties: a memoir of John Gray and André Raffalovich*, London, 1968

Sewell, Brocard, *In the Dorian Mode: a life of John Gray: 1866-1934*, Padstow, 1983

Vernon, Peter, *The Letters of John Gray* (unpublished PhD thesis of the University of London, 1976)

Essays

Bergonzi, Bernard, 'John Gray', in *The Turn of the Century*, London, 1973

Grigson, Geoffrey, 'Dorian Gray/John Gray', in *The Contrary View*, London, 1974

Healy, Philip, 'The Making of an Edinburgh *Salon*', *Journal of the Eighteen Nineties Society*, 1981-2

McCormack, Jerusha, 'The Disciple: John Gray/'Dorian' Gray', *Journal of the Eighteen Nineties Society*, 1975-6

Murray, Isobel, 'John Gray: the person and the work in question', *Durham University Journal*, June 1984

Temple, Ruth Z., 'The Other Choice: the worlds of John Gray, poet and priest', *Bulletin of Research in the Humanities*, 1981